The Case of the Salubrious Soft Coated Wheaten

A Thousand Islands Doggy Inn Mystery

B.R. Snow

Copyright © 2018 B.R. Snow
ISBN: 978-1-942691-52-5

Website: www.brsnow.net/
Twitter: @BernSnow
Facebook: facebook.com/bernsnow

Cover Design: Reggie Cullen
Cover Photo: James R. Miller
Luna Photo: Jim Cummings

Other Books by B.R. Snow

The Thousand Islands Doggy Inn Mysteries

- The Case of the Abandoned Aussie
- The Case of the Brokenhearted Bulldog
- The Case of the Caged Cockers
- The Case of the Dapper Dandie Dinmont
- The Case of the Eccentric Elkhound
- The Case of the Faithful Frenchie
- The Case of the Graceful Goldens
- The Case of the Hurricane Hounds
- The Case of the Itinerant Ibizan
- The Case of the Jaded Jack Russell
- The Case of the Klutz King Charles
- The Case of the Lovable Labs
- The Case of the Mellow Maltese
- The Case of the Natty Newfie
- The Case of the Overdue Otterhound
- The Case of the Prescient Poodle
- The Case of the Quizzical Queens Beagle
- The Case of the Reliable Russian Spaniels

The Whiskey Run Chronicles

- Episode 1 – The Dry Season Approaches
- Episode 2 – Friends and Enemies
- Episode 3 – Let the Games Begin
- Episode 4 – Enter the Revenuer
- Episode 5 – A Changing Landscape
- Episode 6 – Entrepreneurial Spirits
- Episode 7 – All Hands On Deck
- The Whiskey Run Chronicles – The Complete Volume 1
- The Whiskey Run Chronicles – The Complete Volume 2

The Damaged Posse
- American Midnight
- Larrikin Gene
- Sneaker World
- Summerman
- The Duplicates

Other Books

- Divorce Hotel
- Either Ore

For Jim and Mary

And to the memory of Gord Downie

Chapter 1

Wedding week.

After months of intense planning and my mother and I doing everything possible to achieve perfection and anticipate the inevitable what-ifs, not to mention the interminable waiting, mercifully, it has finally arrived. But it's only Tuesday, and I've still got four days to go before I can walk down the aisle and answer the priest's question.

*Do you, Suzy, take Max to be...*well, you know the rest.

And I will respond with confident pride in a loud, clear voice.

"Damn straight, I do."

My mother has threatened to kill me right on the altar if I say it. I know she won't, and she is *almost certain* I would never talk to a priest like that. And I'm *almost certain* I won't. But I am tempted. I know it would get a big laugh as well as give my mother something to complain about at the reception.

Given everything swirling around me at the moment, I'm a wreck. Like a dust-bunny caught in the breeze, I've been unable to maintain control and keep my thoughts from drifting across the emotional spectrum, often before I even realize it's happening. Without warning, joy becomes panic, doubt trumps confidence, animated gives way to forlorn.

And I'm exhausted.

I'm worn out from the minutiae and endless decisions. Worn out by my mother's habit of changing *our* minds and making a few *minor tweaks* to what she'd assured me were the final plans. Worn out from the uncertainty of knowing exactly what's going to happen next as well as what my new life is going to look like going forward. I'm still recovering from our debate about one decision in particular. It should have been easy. A layup in the parlance of people fond of using sports metaphors to make their point.

But as my mother has taught me through the planning process, no detail is too small to not beat to death.

I'm referring to the song Max and I will choose for our first dance, a relatively straightforward decision. But it required extensive negotiations with my mother. The full inventory of our first-dance conversations isn't worth reciting, but to give you an idea, this is how our most recent *chat* went.

"We really need to make a decision on the song, darling."

"Max and I are still discussing it. But don't worry, the band will know what it is before the reception."

"Funny, darling. I think the song should be something traditional."

"Traditional, huh?" I said, raising an eyebrow as I went on point. "Like what?"

"Well, there are so many wonderful choices. How about *At Last* by Etta James?"

"Nah, it's been done to death," I said with a frown.

"Then how about *What A Wonderful World* by Louis Armstrong?"

"Great song. But it's not a good choice for us."

"Okay, let's try something a bit more current," she said. "How about *My Heart Will Go On*?"

"Next."

"What's wrong with it?" my mother said, her agitation ramping up.

"First, it's from *Titanic*. And she's singing to the memory of a dead guy. Second, it's Celine Dion."

"Okay, no Celine Dion. Maybe *As Time Goes By*. Casablanca, dear. One of your favorite movies."

"To watch. Not dance to," I said, making a face as I shook my head. "What else you got?"

"Okay. How about Elvis?" she said. "*Can't Help Falling In Love*. Beautiful song."

"Nah," I said. "Not my favorite Elvis song."

"Then how about *Hard-Headed Woman*?" she deadpanned.

"Funny, Mom. You want to solve the problem or do you want to fight?"

"Keep talking. I'll let you know," she said, scowling at me. "How about *Unforgettable* by Nat King Cole?

"Too slow," I said. "We want to dance."

"Why are you being so difficult?"

"I'm being selective, Mom. There's a difference."

"Okay, your turn. Give me your best shot."

"We were thinking about a Queen song."

"Queen? Not that ridiculous *We Are the Champions*," she said, staring at me in disbelief.

"No. *Another One Bites the Dust*," I deadpanned with a grin.

"Not gonna happen."

"How about a U2 song?"

"I do like U2," she said, nodding.

"I know. How does *I Still Haven't Found What I'm Looking For* grab you?"

"It grabs me by the throat. Just like I'm going to do to you if you don't start taking this seriously. How about *The Way We Were*? Streisand, darling."

"As long as you don't mind me throwing up in my mouth during the whole song."

"*We've Only Just Begun* by the Carpenters?"

I laughed until my stomach hurt.

"I give up. You're impossible," she snapped.

We eventually stuck a pin in *The Way You Look Tonight* by Sinatra and tabled the discussion.

With the wedding on the horizon, major changes are in the air, and dealing with change has never been my strong suit. I like predictability and a sense of order, so when changes do occur I have a solid foundation to fall back on when life begins to tilt, stir or upend. But when the foundation itself begins to shift, I get anxious. Not enough to cause the dreaded *nervous sweats* or induce panic attacks, but I do become edgy. Agitated and oversensitive. And for those around me lately, a total grump.

And at the moment, a little peckish.

I slide an English muffin into the toaster as I stare out the kitchen window at the River. As far as I can see upriver and down, the surface of the water is like glass. It's going to be a warm August day, sweltering if the breeze doesn't kick up, and several folks are already putting their boats through their paces. If I listen closely, I can hear their muffled engines broken only by the occasional cry of a solitary loon or the steady honking of Canadian geese in full flight.

This morning reminds me of hundreds of others I spent on the River as a girl with my mom and dad, as a teen with my year-round friends and summer acquaintances, and, more recently, with Josie and Chef Claire and the dogs. It's going to be one of those perfect summer days in the Islands. The kind you write home about. The kind the Chamber of Commerce prays for by the dozen. And if things unfold the way they might, like my wedding, it's the kind of day you'll remember forever.

I choke up as the wave begins to build. Memories have been flooding back in recent weeks. And the older I get, I must admit to feeling overwhelmed at times by an inescapable wave of melancholy. It's not an overpowering feeling provoking despair. It's more of a not-so-gentle reminder of good times gone, times incapable of being recreated due to age and changing

5

circumstances, yet still tucked away in my memory bank to be called upon when needed. Or surfacing at times when certain memories are the last thing you want to be dealing with.

The melancholy, a somewhat new experience for me, arrived in fits and starts a few months ago then increased in frequency and intensity as the day of celebration neared. And when it did, I began forcing it into our work and dinner conversations. I've played far too many games of *Do you remember the time when...?* I've remembered, reminisced, recounted and replayed until my head hurt. I've laughed and cried, told long stories, and had even longer conversations with myself. And it's not like I don't know all the maxims. The proverbs of providence. Time marches on. All things must pass. There must be dozens, and I'm sure I've used them all over the course of the past several weeks.

Melancholy.

What a powerful emotion. When used well, it can provide sweet reminders of a life well led. Used incorrectly it can induce an overwhelming sense of dread and crippling fear about the future.

My melancholy began to dominate and play out on a daily basis until, one night over dinner, Josie finally hit the wall. She put her knife and fork down in mid-meal, a rare occurrence, glanced at Chef Claire, who nodded her agreement it was time, then fixed a hard stare on me.

"For God sake, Suzy. Will you please knock it off? We're only moving *two hundred feet* down the street."

From that point on, convinced my foundation would remain rock-solid, I began to relax and do my best to enjoy the change process.

The dogs also sense change is in the air and something is afoot. Josie and Chef Claire moving down the street will mean Chloe, my Australian Shepherd, will also be losing her permanent housemates. Captain, Josie's Newfie, and Al and Dente, Chef Claire's Golden Retrievers, will also be moving out. I keep waiting for signs of distress from Chloe letting me know she is troubled by the idea, but she's apparently handling the move a lot better than I am.

At the moment all four of them look anything other than stressed out. They're in the reception area of the Doggy Inn rolling around on the floor. The object in question is a rope toy with a large knot on each end and Captain has it trapped underneath him. Given his massive size, it's hidden from view. But the other three dogs are determined to find it. Before long, a section of the rope pops into view and Chloe and the Goldens seize their opportunity. They grab it and begin pulling hard. Captain holds the toy with his front paws and slides a knotted end into his mouth. He effortlessly holds the toy while the other three dogs wear them themselves out trying to get it from him. Captain seems amused by their futile efforts and glances back and forth at them, his tail wagging the entire time. Only Chloe's

7

stealth move of pulling one of Captain's ears breaks the stalemate.

Josie and I watch the scene play out from behind the reception counter laughing the entire time.

"He's so strong," I said, marveling at the Newfie.

"He gets it from his mother," Josie said, gently punching me on the shoulder. "Are you feeling better this morning?"

"I am. It's no big deal, right?" I said, shrugging. "You guys are only moving down the street."

"And Chloe can sleep over anytime she wants," Josie said, laughing again as Captain manages to get both knots of the rope toy in his mouth.

Soon, all four dogs have a piece of the rope in their mouth and are pulling hard. Chloe's nails click against the linoleum as she gives a mighty tug and lets loose with a low playful, guttural growl. But Captain has the upper hand, and Chloe concedes with a snort. She lets go of the toy and heads for the registration counter and hops up on a chair where she sits staring at me with a front paw raised. I return the handshake and rub her head.

"He's too strong, isn't he?" I said sympathetically.

"I don't want it."

Josie shakes her head at Captain after he proudly strolls to the counter still holding the rope toy in his mouth. It's become a slobbery mess, and he cocks his head at his mother. At first glance, it might appear he's offering the toy to her as some sort of gift. But we both know Captain is merely trying to tempt Josie into a tugging match, a battle she knows from experience she can't win. Josie grins as she shakes her head again at the Newfie.

"No way. I'm not touching that. It's disgusting."

Captain drops the toy to woof at Josie. Al and Dente seize their opportunity and move in to snatch it off the floor. Al ends up with sole possession, and he races toward the condo area in the back of the Inn with Captain and Dente in hot pursuit. Chloe, not wanting to miss out, hops from the chair onto the counter then launches herself through the air. She lands softly and dashes off without missing a beat and follows the other three into the condo area.

"I get tired watching them," Josie said.

"Me too," I said. "I'm gonna count it."

Josie gives me another soft punch on the shoulder, and we both glance at the front door when it opens. One of our favorite dogs and two of our favorite people step inside. Luna, a beautiful Soft Coated Wheaten Terrier, heads straight for the reception counter and hops on her back legs with her front paws gently scratching the outside of the counter. Josie and I lean forward and peer down at her. Luna wags what tail she has vigorously and judging by the look of anticipation on her face is expecting Josie and me to come around the counter and say hi. We immediately comply.

"Hey, Luna," I said, returning the hug she is giving me. "Who's the good girl?"

Luna licks my face several times then turns her attention to Josie who is now sitting on the floor. Luna launches herself into Josie's lap and gives her dozens of kisses. Several moments later, Luna is satisfied with the greeting and focuses on Jim and Mary Cummings who've been watching the scene play out with smiles and the occasional shake of their heads. Jim and Mary always board Luna at the Inn when they need to leave town and can't take her with them. They are not merely dog owners; they are *dog people*. And those of you who spend a lot of time with our four-legged friends know exactly what I'm talking about. Those of you not blessed with canine-companionship may not see the distinction, but the difference is wide and deep.

"Somebody's excited to be here," Josie said, climbing to her feet.

"She's been excited since we asked her last night if she wanted to go the Inn," Mary said, kneeling down to pet the Wheatie.

"Yeah," Jim deadpanned. "I don't think she got more than ten, maybe twelve hours of sleep last night."

"Oh, stop," Mary said. Then she focused on me. "How are you holding up? The big day is right around the corner."

"I'm doing good," I said, sitting down in a chair. Luna is soon occupying my lap. "But don't tell my mom. As long as I can keep her believing I'm stressed out, she goes easy on me. It's one of the rare times I get the upper hand."

Jim and Mary laugh along with Josie and me. They sit down across from me, and Luna glances back and forth at their laps before deciding on Jim's.

"I pulled Luna's chart this morning," Josie said. "She's due for her rabies."

"She is," Mary said. "And could you clip her nails and groom her?"

"Already got it written down," Josie said, sitting down next to me. "She'll be here the one night, right?"

"Yeah," Jim said. "We're heading up to Montreal to pick up Geraldine. She's flying in from L.A. tonight. We're going to do some sightseeing and shopping before she gets in."

"I can't wait to see her," I said. "It's been way too long."

"Yeah, she doesn't get back much," Mary said. "Family, huh?"

"She still fighting with her dad?" I said.

"Only when she's in the same room with him," Mary said with a small smile. "I was surprised when she told us she was coming in for the wedding."

Geraldine was a childhood friend I went to school with. We'd been close, but she had moved with her mom to the west coast after her parents split up. Her brother, Billy, had stayed in Clay Bay with his dad. But several years ago, after finishing college, he'd left the area for New York to pursue an acting career. From what we've heard, he's been a moderate success, which probably means he's earning enough to survive and afford living in the City.

"Since Billy and Geraldine are coming in for the wedding, we thought we'd have a family dinner at our place tomorrow night," Mary said. "Why don't you guys stop by? It will be a good chance for you to catch up with some folks you haven't seen in a while."

"Sounds great, Mary," I said. "And tomorrow night is open."

"Perfect. It should be fun," Mary said. Her comment got a snort out of Jim. Mary glared at her husband. "Stop. It's going to be fine. Everyone has promised to be on their best behavior."

"And you believed them?" Jim said.

"Knock it off," Mary said, stifling a laugh. "Josie, why don't you and Chef Claire come along?" Mary said. "You've never met most of my family."

"No, I've only met you and Charlie," Josie said. "Sure, it sounds like fun."

"Perfect," Jim said. "Any time after six is great."

"Casual, right?" I said.

"I'd go with a referee's shirt," Jim said, grinning at his wife. "And don't forget your whistle."

"You're really not funny, Jim," Mary said, shaking her head.

"Are you guys going to be able to make it to the wedding?" I said. "My mom has you down as a maybe."

"We were able to move some stuff around. We're definitely going to be there," Jim said.

Jim and Mary are the caretakers at Twilight Island, home of Dancer Castle, a medieval-looking structure of around forty rooms and, according to local folklore, filled with hidden entrances to secret passageways. The castle had recently undergone renovations and during the day now offered visitor tours. It was also possible to rent the castle's wedding suite for overnight stays. When my mother first suggested Max and I spent our wedding night there, I wondered if she'd lost her mind. But after talking it over, we came around to the idea.

After the wedding reception, we'll head to the island by boat, spend the evening there, then be picked up at the island the next morning by a private yacht. The boat, equipped with a captain, a chef, and a handful of other crew members will take us on a leisurely tour down the St. Lawrence River to Montreal. Our plan is to spend a few days in the city, one of our favorites, before flying off to Paris for ten days.

I had to give my mother credit. She's put together a great itinerary for us, and we're looking forward to our honeymoon. Not to mention the rest of our lives together.

"When are you and Chef Claire moving in?" Jim said, rubbing Luna's head.

"We've already started moving some of our things in," Josie said, then glanced at Mary. "Your uncle said he was getting the last of his stuff out today."

"Yeah, he is," she said. "We stopped by before we came here. He said he was almost done. We offered to help him, but he's stubborn. What a shock, huh?" She laughed. "When we left, he was about to head up to the attic to pack the last of his memorabilia. And he won't let anybody touch his stuff."

"He's in the attic?" Josie said. "What the heck is he thinking? The guy's in his nineties."

"I know," Jim said. "But he's adamant it's something he needs to do."

"At least he agreed not to carry any boxes down the stairs," Mary said. "He promised to leave them for the movers."

"He's going into assisted living?" I said.

"He is," Mary said. "He's still not thrilled about it, but it's too hard for him to live in the house by himself. Especially in the winter. But he did say he's happy you bought the house. Says it relaxes him knowing it's going to be in good hands."

"Chef Claire and I will take good care of it," Josie said.

"Is there anything special you and Max would like at the island?" Jim said. "I can't imagine you're going to be hungry after the reception."

"Not so fast, Jim," Josie said.

"Don't start," I said, laughing. "I can't think of anything, Jim. I think my mom had a couple bottles of champagne delivered."

"She did. They're in the fridge at the castle," Mary said. "And she also ordered some stuff to snack on."

"I love your mom," Josie said, grinning. "She thinks of everything."

"It's a little hard for her to forget food and drink," I said. "Especially with you nagging her."

"I don't nag," Josie said, reaching for Luna. "I *remind*. Okay, Luna. Say goodbye to your mama and papa, and we'll go get you settled in." She cuddled the Wheaten in her arms. "I'll see you guys tomorrow night. And I'll also see you at the wedding. I'll be the one holding the bride up to keep her from fainting."

"Funny," I said.

Chapter 2

I set the box I was carrying down in the middle of the living room then sprawled out in one of the overstuffed chairs next to the fireplace. Josie sat down in a chair next to me and took a long pull from a bottle of cold water.

"I think that's enough for now," Josie said, glancing around the room. "I'll start unboxing all this crap tomorrow."

A loud round of clangs and bangs came from the kitchen, and we both laughed.

"She said she was going to get started on the kitchen," Josie said, then called out. "Hey, Chef Claire."

Moments later, Chef Claire wearing shorts and a tee shirt and a bandana wrapped around her head appeared in the doorway.

"Am I being too loud?" she said.

"Maybe a little," Josie said. "C'mon, take a break. It's gonna take us days to get settled in."

"Well, you know me," Chef Claire said. "I need my kitchen."

"Yes, we know," Josie said. "And we are all the better for that. But have a seat and relax."

"I'll sit down in a few minutes," Chef Claire said. "I want to head upstairs and check to see how Charlie is doing.

16

"I haven't heard a peep out of him since we got here," I said. "What's he still doing up there?"

"He said he has a few more things to box up," Chef Claire said. "I think the idea of leaving the house has finally hit him."

"After sixty years, it has to be," I said.

"I hate the thought of him going up and down that ladder and rummaging around the attic," Chef Claire said.

"He's pretty spry. What is he, ninety-one?" Josie said.

"Ninety-two," Chef Claire said, heading for the stairs. "I'm going to check on him. I'll be right back."

"It's a great house," I said, glancing around.

"Yeah, I like it," Josie said. "It won't be the same, but it's still good, right?"

"I guess," I said.

A blood-curdling scream came from the second floor, and we scrambled out of our chairs and up the stairs. We found Chef Claire standing over the body of Charlie Merrihew. He was sprawled out at the bottom of a collapsible ladder. A collection of war memorabilia was scattered around the floor. A pool of blood had formed, and he had a cut on his neck. Chef Claire knelt down next to the body, checked for signs of a pulse then shook her head in despair. She sat down next to him and began to sob.

"I didn't hear a peep out of him," Chef Claire said. "I was making a racket in the kitchen. I'm so sorry, Charlie."

17

"Don't beat yourself up. It's not your fault," I said. "We didn't hear anything either, and we were sitting a lot closer to the stairs." I frowned. "It seems odd we didn't hear him fall."

"Maybe he fell earlier while we were carrying in all the boxes," Josie said.

"Yeah, I suppose it's possible," I said, leaning close but not touching the body.

"Oh, Charlie. You poor guy," Chef Claire finally managed. "He must have fallen off the ladder, and something in the box fell out and stabbed him."

"It was probably that thing," Josie said, pointing at what looked like a bayonet. "Yeah, there's definitely blood on it."

I grabbed my phone and made a call.

"Hey, Chief," I said. "Look, I hate to ruin your afternoon, but we have a problem over here. No, not the Inn. The Merrihew place. It's Charlie." I listened and nodded. "Yeah, he's gone. You'll see when you get here…No, we haven't touched anything. Chef Claire checked for a pulse, but nothing else. Okay, see you soon."

I slid my phone back into my shorts and grimaced as I stared down at the dead man's face. I'd known Charlie since I was a little girl and he was what many people referred to as *colorful*. Friendly, but prone to turning cranky in a hurry, especially with members of his family. He loved to chat but often fell silent when the conversation veered into what he considered overly personal. Overall, he was a good guy who

18

deserved to go out in a better way than falling off a ladder and getting stabbed in the neck by a piece of war memorabilia.

"Geez," Josie said, sitting down on the floor with her back pressed up against the wall. "What are the odds of that happening?"

"Gotta be a million to one, right?" I said, sneaking a quick peek at Charlie's wound. Then I worked my way across the floor on my knees and sat next to Josie.

"What the heck was he thinking trying to carry the box down the ladder?" Chef Claire said.

"Stubborn and independent," Josie said. "Probably not a good combination when you're in your nineties."

"I can't believe it. Charlie's gone. He was like an institution around town," I said.

"He told us some great stories while we were negotiating on the house," Josie said. "He had a bunch of them about where he picked up some of his memorabilia."

"We couldn't be sure, but it sounded like he got five-finger discounts on some of the stuff."

"He stole it?" I said, surprised.

"Yeah, I think so," Chef Claire said. "It sure sounded like it."

"It did," Josie said, nodding. "He swore up and down most of his family weren't getting squat."

19

"He called them vultures," Chef Claire said, managing a small smile. "Birds of prey hanging around waiting for him to kick the bucket. He swore he was gonna outlive all of them."

We heard the sound of a car pulling into the driveway. Chef Claire headed for the stairs.

"That'll be the Chief," she said. "I'll let him in."

She bounded down the stairs. Josie shook her head again at the body.

"After everything he did in life, he goes out by falling off a ladder and getting stabbed in the neck by a bayonet," she said, then glanced over at me. "You ever think about how you might die?"

"Now, there's a cheery thought," I said. "Not really. But I hope it's not a violent death. Maybe go in my sleep."

"No, not me," Josie said. "I want to know when I'm going. Dying has to be the ultimate life experience, right?"

"I guess it's one way to look at it," I said, frowning. "I don't spend a lot of time thinking about it. How do you see it happening?"

"I don't know," she said. "Maybe a food overdose."

"One too many trips through the buffet line?"

"There you go. Hey, Chief. Freddie."

"Good afternoon, ladies," Chief Abrams said, immediately focused on Charlies' body.

"How are you doing?" Freddie, our local medical examiner, said to us before focusing on his work. He knelt down, checked

20

for signs of a pulse then shook his head at our chief of police. "Ah, Charlie. Poor guy. What the heck happened?"

"It looks like he was trying to carry the box down from the attic and fell off the ladder. There's an old bayonet on the floor near the body. It must have stabbed him in the neck," I said.

"Talk about your bad luck," Freddie said, studying the body and position of the bayonet.

"I hate seeing this," Chief Abrams said, shaking his head. "I always liked Charlie."

"It looks like it might have nicked his jugular," Freddie said. "He would have bled out pretty quickly."

"And you guys didn't hear anything?" Chief Abrams said.

"No, we were downstairs unpacking boxes," Josie said.

"Okay," the Chief said, getting to his feet. "Who in his family is still living in town?"

"I think Mary Cummings is the only one who's local," I said. "Charlie was her uncle. But his kids are coming in for the wedding."

"Billy and Geraldine, right?" the Chief said.

"Yeah," I said.

"I know he's an actor," the Chief said. "What does she do?"

"She's some sort of antiquities consultant," I said. "I don't have a clue what it means other than she deals with rare, old things."

"Then she's gonna love you, Chief," Freddie said, glancing over his shoulder at Chief Abrams with a grin.

21

"Really?" the Chief said. "You're taking a shot at me for being old?"

"I was referring to the *rare* comment," Freddie said, still grinning.

"Yeah, I'm sure you were," the Chief said. "Why don't you do your thing so we can get him out of here." Chief Abrams shook his head at the ME then his knees popped. He groaned when he got to his feet. "Not a word, Freddie."

"I rest my case," Freddie said. "Okay, I think I've seen all I need to for the moment. I'll get him back to my place for a closer look. But it's definitely going down as accidental. Wrong place, wrong time, doing something dumb. But I'll let you know if I find anything noteworthy."

"Thanks," Chief Abrams said, then turned to me. "When are Charlie's kids getting in?"

"I think Billy is coming in today. And Jim and Mary headed up to Montreal this afternoon to pick Geraldine up at the airport."

"I'll give Mary a call and ask her to break the news to the daughter. Hopefully, she has Billy's number. They need to know what happened to their old man before they get here."

"Okay, Chief," I said. "I should know the answer to this, but I can't keep up. Are you coming to dinner tonight?"

"You mean the pre-rehearsal-dinner dinner?" he said, laughing.

"You got it," I said, laughing along. "This one is pretty much friends and family. At least it was yesterday. How about you, Freddie?"

"I'll be there," he said. "What are we having?"

"Lots of good stuff," Chef Claire said. "Come hungry."

"I'll do my best," Josie deadpanned.

"Now there's a surprise," Chef Claire said. "And Freddie, since Josie will be there, you might want to come early."

Chapter 3

I paused long enough from my dinner to lean over and give Max a quick kiss on the cheek. He squeezed my thigh then pulled me in close for a hug.

"How's your dinner?" I said, refocusing on my pasta.

"Incredible. As always," Max said, taking a sip of wine. "I'm going to gain a ton of weight if I keep eating like this. Will you still love me after I get fat?"

"All you need to do is start hanging out at the Inn," I said. "You'll get plenty of exercise wrangling the dogs."

"You didn't answer my question."

"Oh, you caught that," I said. "Yes, I think I'll be able to deal with it."

"You sure you don't some wine?" Max said.

"No, thanks," I said, shaking my head. "Wine doesn't sound good tonight."

"More for me," he said, laughing as he got up from the table. "I'll be right back."

Max slid his chair back, somehow managed to get his pant leg caught on the bottom of the chair and toppled hard to the floor. There's one thing you should know about my fiancé. He's an even bigger klutz than I am. Max is constantly bumping his head, banging his knees and elbows, and bouncing off doorways.

Somehow, especially when he gets excited, Max often finds a way to do damage to himself.

"Are you okay?" I said, watching as he climbed to his feet.

"Yeah, I'm fine," he said, red-faced. "How the heck did I manage that one?"

"You need an escort to the bathroom?" I said. "You know, in case you get lost. Or fall in."

"Funny," Max said, making a face at me before heading off.

"He hurts himself a lot," Freddie said as he watched Max's departure. "Try to keep him safe and sound on the honeymoon."

"He does make me look like a ballerina," I said. "Did you get a chance to take a good look at Charlie?"

"Yeah," Freddie said. "I still can't believe he's gone. He was a bit of a curmudgeon, but I loved the guy."

"Yeah, me too," I said, slowly chewing a piece of chicken. "How long do you think he was up there before we found him.

"It looks like he probably fell off the ladder an hour or two before you guys found him," Freddie said. "The puncture wound was pretty deep. Hopefully, he went quick."

"Yeah, let's hope so," I said, then frowned. "Did you say the puncture wound was deep?"

"I did," Freddie said. "What about it?"

I drifted off for a moment as I tried to recall what I'd seen earlier. I'd been kneeling down to take a close look at Charlie. But there was so much blood I hadn't gotten a good look at the wound. A question bubbled inside my head and I frowned. All of a sudden something wasn't gelling for me. I must have had an odd look on my face because Freddie stared at me. Chief Abrams, sitting across the table from me, also noticed.

"What's the matter?" Chief Abrams said.

"I don't know," Freddie said. "But she's got the look."

"It's odd," I said.

"What's odd?" Freddie said.

"When I first saw Charlie's body, I assumed his neck had been slit. And I could understand the bayonet doing all that damage if it sliced Charlie's throat. But from what you said, it sounds like it was more of a stab wound."

"Yeah, it definitely went pretty deep. But the bayonet is sharp. I'm not following you, Suzy," Freddie said as he continued to attack his dinner.

"How wide was the puncture wound?" the Chief said, apparently picking up on where I was going.

Freddie held up his pinkie finger then took another bite.

"It was pretty narrow. But the width wasn't the issue," Freddie said. "It was the depth of the wound that killed him."

Chief Abrams and I shared a long, intense stare. Freddie noticed and set his knife and fork down. He wiped his mouth and took a sip of water as he glanced back and forth at us.

"What am I missing?" Freddie said.

"How deep was the wound?" Chief Abrams said.

"About two and a half inches," he said, now edgy. "What the heck is going on with you two?"

26

"Think it through, Freddie," the Chief said.

"There's nothing to think about, Chief," Freddie said, grabbing his fork. "The guy did a header off the ladder, dropped the box he was carrying, and the bayonet landed on him with the point facing down. You said it yourself earlier. It was a million to one shot."

Chief Abrams and I shook our heads in tandem.

"If Charlie had been stabbed with the bayonet, the wound would have been wider," I said.

Freddie processed my comment then he glanced back and forth at us with a dazed expression.

"Geez," Freddie said. "I can't believe I missed it. As soon as we put it down as an accident, I barely paid any attention to connecting the dots between the wound and the bayonet. And the bayonet was covered in blood. Man, I need to lift my game. I'm totally embarrassed."

"Maybe old age is creeping up on you," Chief Abrams deadpanned.

"Funny, Chief. But you might be right," Freddie said, shaking his head. "I completely whiffed. I can't believe it."

"Don't beat yourself up," I said.

"Yeah, that's my job," Chief Abrams said.

"The puncture wound came from a narrower blade," I stated.

"Yeah, it must have," Freddie said, still stunned by his oversight. "If I keep this up, I'm going to have to turn in my ME card. Geez, how could I have been so sloppy?"

"We all assumed it was an accident," I said.

"Yeah," the Chief said. "How could it have been anything different?"

"And if the bayonet didn't create the wound, why the heck was it covered in blood?" My frown deepened.

"Great minds think alike," Chief Abrams said. "You think this whole thing might have been staged to look like an accident?"

"Yeah, as weird as it sounds, I think I do," I said, still having a hard time believing it.

"How is that even possible?" Josie said, joining the conversation. "We were downstairs the entire time."

"We'd only been there about an hour. And we were carrying boxes into the house most of the time," I said, then turned to Freddie. "You said Charlie could have been dead for an hour or two before we found him."

"Yeah, but I need to take another look. Since I've made such a mess of things," Freddie said.

"Okay, Freddie," Josie said. "You've confessed you whiffed on this one, but enough is enough. We all screw up at work. Let it go."

"Sorry," Freddie said. "But it's pretty basic stuff."

"This means we could be looking at murder here," the Chief said. "But who the heck did it? And how did they manage to get in and out of the house without you noticing?"

"Maybe they were in the attic the whole time," Chef Claire said.

"Oh, now there's a cheery thought," Josie said, shaking her head. "Some psychopath has decided to squat in our attic."

"I need to go check out the house," Chief Abrams said, getting to his feet.

"Don't you want to finish your dinner first?" I said.

"No, I need to take care of this," the Chief said. "But ask your folks to keep it warm if you don't mind."

"Will do," Chef Claire said.

"You guys stay here at the restaurant until I get back, okay?"

"You got it, Chief," Josie said.

"I'm coming with you," Freddie said, also getting to his feet.

We watched them head for the exit. My mother noticed their departure and looked at me.

"Where are they going?" she said.

"It looks like Charlie's death wasn't an accident," I said.

"What?"

"Yeah," I said. "He might have been murdered."

"I don't believe it. Why on earth would anyone want to kill Charlie?" she said, then glanced at Paulie.

29

"It doesn't make any sense," Paulie said with a frown.

"No, it doesn't," she said, then gave me the evil eye. "Please promise me you'll behave yourself the rest of the week, darling. We do have quite a bit at stake here."

"Sure, sure."

"I mean it, young lady," she said. "Your only priority is the wedding. Am I making myself clear?"

"Yes, Mother," I said, chastised.

"Good," she said, nodding.

"We haven't even moved in yet and somebody has already been killed?" Josie said, shaking her head.

"Who'd want to kill Charlie?" Chef Claire said. "He was a good guy. A little grumpy from time to time, but he was a sweetheart."

"He was," I said. "It doesn't make any sense. Somebody comes into the house and decides to kill him while he's cleaning out his attic?"

"Yeah, it's nuts," Chef Claire said.

"Well, you have been saying you're looking for something to take your mind off the stress of the wedding," Josie said.

"Yeah, but this isn't what I had in mind," I said.

"No, I'm sure it's not," she said. "But it oughta do the trick."

Chapter 4

I've known the Merrihew family for as long as I can remember. Charlie Merrihew, the now deceased patriarch, was a tough, no-nonsense sort of guy who'd expected a lot from himself and even more from his kids. He'd somehow managed to enlist in the Army at the age of fourteen right after the bombing of Pearl Harbor and had served honorably in both Europe and the Pacific. Like many other veterans, Charlie didn't like to talk about his war years. Apart from his propensity to regale anyone who would listen to his stories about the memorabilia he had *discovered* during his years overseas and the manner by which they came into his possession. Discovered was Charlie's term. It certainly wasn't the word his wife Margaret had used to describe the boxes of *unmitigated junk* filling her attic for the majority of their marriage.

After the war, his search for additional objects to add to his collection continued and he regularly made the rounds of garage and estate sales hoping to uncover even more items. But it was their divorce coinciding with the explosion of the Internet that spun Charlie's passion for historical artifacts into orbit. And after Mary got him a personal computer for his 80th birthday, Charlie developed an impressive set of computer skills that rivaled those of many local kids who'd grown up with technology.

Geraldine, sitting on a couch chatting with Max, had done her best to follow in her father's footsteps. She'd studied archeology, spent time in Europe, the Middle East, and several Pacific islands where, as she had spent the past half-hour trying to explain, developed a lucrative business as a memorabilia broker. I didn't completely understand what she did, but it sounded like people hired her to travel the world in search of specific antiquities they wanted to get their hands on.

She worked hard to earn her father's praise but often had to settle for grudging respect. But it was a lot better than what her brother, Billy Merrihew, ever got from their father. When Billy announced at an early age his intention to become an actor his father made his contempt for the idea perfectly clear. *Utter nonsense*, he had said, dismissing his son's career choice as the ultimate in bad decisions.

Geraldine was in my class all throughout school, and we'd been good friends. But after she finished college, she headed off to *find herself,* and we'd drifted apart. I hadn't seen her for several years, and when she promptly accepted the invitation to the wedding, I was surprised and delighted. I was even more shocked when Billy had made the decision to attend since his trips back to Clay Bay were even rarer than his sister's. He'd been a year behind me in school, and I'd always found him to be a gentle soul with a ton of creative talent. At the moment he was leaning against a doorway chatting with his girlfriend, a woman by the name of Séance, an actress with an annoying, *delicate* personality and an ego that filled the room. When she'd introduced herself about an hour ago, she had extended her hand and slowly pronounced her name. But when my face didn't light up in immediate recognition, she took her hand back and scowled at my obviously philistine sensibilities.

I spotted Jim and Mary chatting with Chef Claire on the patio and made my way outside. I sat down, and Luna immediately hopped up on my lap to say hello.

"Just tell her to get down," Mary said, laughing as she watched the Wheatey lick the side of my face.

"Now why would I want to do that?" I said, rubbing the dog's head. "She's such a good girl."

Luna spotted a couple of people sitting in front of a tray of appetizers and hopped down. She headed straight for them in search of a snack.

"She's something else," I said, shaking my head at the dog who was already on her haunches and glancing back and forth at the two snackers. "What's the word you use to describe her?"

"Salubrious," Jim said.

"Good word," Chef Claire said. "Beneficial. Promoting a healthy life, right?"

"Well, look at you. A chef and a scholar," Jim said, raising his wine glass in salute. "But the word works with most dogs, right?"

"You'll get no argument from us," I said, taking a sip of iced tea.

"What's the Graverobber up to?" Jim said.

"Jim," Mary said, laughing. "Don't start."

"It's what she does," he said with a shrug. "When she's not changing her travel plans and forgetting to let anybody know."

Chef Claire and I both frowned at the comment then glanced back and forth at them waiting for clarification.

"You know how we were saying yesterday we had to drive to Montreal to pick Geraldine up?" Mary said.

"Yeah," I said, nodding.

"Well, she decided not to fly into Montreal," Mary said.

"Where did she land?" I said.

"Toronto," Jim said, shaking his head. "Of course, she neglected to tell us. Well, I hope she enjoyed her drive down."

"I take it you guys didn't pick her up," I said.

"Uh, no," Jim said. "Typical Geraldine."

"You need to go easy on her, Jim," Mary said. "She did lose her father yesterday."

"Yeah, I know," he said softly. "But it would have only taken a phone call."

"Why the change in plans?" I said.

"She wanted to see *Hamilton*," he said. "Apparently she has a friend who's in the touring company. They've started a run in Toronto."

"How did she take the news when you told her about Charlie?" I said. "I talked with her earlier, but she wasn't ready to go into it."

"She's pretty much like the rest of us," Mary said. "Uncle Charlie was getting up there, so the fact he died didn't come as a total shock. But the idea somebody killed him is…"

Mary teared up, and Jim draped an arm over her shoulder.

"I'm sorry," she said.

"Don't worry about it, Mary," Chef Claire said. "It has to be devastating."

"I can't believe anybody would want to hurt Uncle Charlie," Mary said.

Jim frowned and looked away, but Mary caught his expression.

"What?" she said. "You got something to say?"

"I can think of a few suspects," Jim said, glancing around the backyard where several members of the extended Merrihew family were chatting with each other. A conversation between Charlie's two brothers appeared to be heating up. "There was only one member of your family who took the time to help Charlie out. And we both know who it was."

"I loved Uncle Charlie," Mary said. "I was happy to do everything I could. And I'm the only one in the family who lives in town."

"Yeah, I know," Jim said. "But still. At a minimum, Billy and Geraldine could have made an occasional appearance."

"I agree with you when it comes to Geraldine," Mary said. "But Billy is a different matter."

"How so?" Chef Claire said.

"Billy and Uncle Charlie had been estranged for years," Mary said. "Charlie didn't approve of Billy's decision to go into acting."

"That's it?" Chef Claire said, frowning. "His son decided to pursue his passion and his father cut him off?"

"Pretty much," Mary said. "Uncle Charlie said acting wasn't *man's* work."

"And scrounging around estate sales trying to find World War II junk was?" Jim said, shaking his head.

"They had a complicated relationship," Mary said.

"The kid never had a shot with his old man," Jim said. "Charlie could never accept the fact his only son wasn't cut from the same cloth as he was."

"Billy looks good," I said. "I can't remember the last time I saw him."

"He does," Jim said. "And he seems happy. He should be congratulated, not condemned for getting away from this collection of so-called family."

"Jim, please stop," Mary said.

"No, I'm not going to stop, Mary. You took great care of Charlie for all those years, and the only thing you ever got from those people were questions about your real motives," Jim said, shaking his head. "It was shabby treatment. Downright shabby."

"And now he's gone," Mary said, again tearing up. "I can't believe anybody could do that to a man in his nineties."

"It's despicable," Chef Claire said.

"Yeah, despicable is the word," Jim said, then decided a new topic of conversation was called for. "Hey, I saw you talking with Séance earlier. She's delightful, huh?"

"She's something else," Chef Claire said. "At first, she thought I was joking when I told her I'd never heard of her."

"Ouch," Mary said. "That's like a dagger to the heart for her." Then she thought about what she'd said and frowned. "Sorry. Bad choice of words."

"According to Billy, she's having a tough time finding work in New York," Jim said. "Nobody wants to work with her."

"Really?" Chef Claire said. "She told me she recently finished an extended run of an off-Broadway show."

"That's what she said?" Jim said, laughing. "Off-Broadway?"

"Yeah, why is that funny?" Chef Claire said.

"I guess it depends," Jim said, still laughing. "On whether or not Cleveland fits your definition of off-Broadway."

"Now *that's* funny," Chef Claire said.

"I meant to ask you," I said. "How did all the family end up here at the same time? They must have all made their plans before they knew anything had happened to Charlie."

"It was my idea," Mary said. "As soon as I heard Billy and Geraldine were coming in for your wedding, I thought it might be a nice idea to try to get the family together."

"Who are they all?" I said, glancing around the yard. "I recognize a couple of your aunts and uncles."

"Mostly cousins and their spouses," she said.

Geraldine approached and plopped down in a chair, apparently exhausted. Jim got to his feet and drained the last of his beer.

"I need to go check on dinner," he said, avoiding eye contact with Geraldine.

"I'll give you a hand," Mary said.

Geraldine watched them head off, trailed by Luna, then shook her head.

"He's still mad at me for not letting him know I'd changed my travel plans," she said.

"So you drove in from Toronto?" I said.

"I did. I'd forgotten how long a drive it is."

"How was *Hamilton*?" Chef Claire said.

"A-ma-zing," Geraldine said, drifting off for a moment. "Despite the drive, it was worth the effort."

"I'm so sorry about what happened to your Dad," Chef Claire said.

"Thank you," she said softly. "But he had a nice long run."

"An awful way to go out," I said.

"Yes, it was," she said, then teared up. "Do the police really think somebody killed him?"

"They think it's definitely a possibility," I said. "But it makes no sense. Why would anybody want to do that to your dad?"

"I have no idea," Geraldine said with a sad shrug as she wiped her eyes. "Dad could be difficult, but it certainly wasn't any reason to kill him. I've spent the last several hours trying to come up with a motive."

"Love and money are always pretty high on the list," I said.

"I doubt anybody killed Dad over love," Geraldine said, then drifted off for a moment. "Lack of love maybe."

I flinched at her comment but said nothing.

"And I can't imagine anybody did it for money," she said.

"Apart from the house, he didn't have a lot, did he?" I said.

"If he did, nobody knew it," Geraldine said, shaking her head.

I flinched again and frowned. But before I had a chance to follow up, I heard Max's voice coming from the top of the patio steps.

"There you are," he said, waving to me.

Max, mid-step, turned to return the wave of a man standing nearby and caught the back of his foot on the top step. He windmilled his arms to catch his balance to no avail. He tumbled down the stairs, bounced a couple of times and landed hard on his on his elbows.

"Geez, Max, are you okay?" I said, heading his way.

"Yeah, I'll be fine. Apart from feeling like a complete idiot," he said, pushing himself to his feet and examining the scrapes on his elbows. "That hurt."

"You better take it easy," I said, gently turning both arms to examine the bruises. "I don't think they make body casts in formal wear."

"Funny. And I'm only on my second beer," he said, grimacing. "I'll be fine. Jim and Mary sent me out to let everybody know dinner's ready."

"Then let's go eat," I said, hooking my arm inside his. "C'mon, follow me. I'll make sure you get to the table without breaking a leg."

"You're on fire tonight," he said, squeezing my hand. "And to think I've got a whole lifetime ahead of me to enjoy your dazzling wit."

"Yeah, you are a lucky man, aren't you?"

Chapter 5

Over the years, given my mother's ability to push my buttons and drive me up the wall of her choosing, I've gotten pretty good at recognizing and dealing with family dynamics. But the Merrihew clan appeared to have their own version that was hard for me as an outsider to fully comprehend. There appeared to be an unspoken demarcation line dividing the dinner table in half. At the far end, Jim and Mary sat with Charlie's two brothers and his sister. All three of them were living alone either via divorce or widowhood, and their conversations were conducted in hushed yet somewhat hostile tones. It quickly became apparent any shared sense of grief had given way to their shared history, and it was impossible to miss the fact Charlie's siblings, while not having been a big fan of him, cared even less for each other.

A group of the extended family, primarily cousins and their offspring, were sitting on lawn chairs arranged in the backyard below the patio where we were sitting. Their conversations were sporadic and seemed to consist of comments about how good the food was or questions designed to bring everyone up to speed about what had been going on in their lives since the last time they had gotten together and asked each other pretty much the same set of questions.

At our end of the table, I was sitting with Charlie's two kids. Billy and Séance were across from me and engaged in a whispered conversation. The actress was nodding at something Billy was saying through a glazed stare.

"She looks out of it," I whispered to Josie. "Has she been hitting the wine hard?"

"No, I think it's chemically-induced," she whispered back. "I saw her pop some pills about an hour ago."

"Prescription drugs?"

"Well, I don't think they were M&Ms."

The couple's conversation heated up. Soon, their hostile stares had me fighting every eavesdropping urge in my repertoire. Max, sensing my growing interest, gently patted my thigh under the table. And when his touch didn't produce the result he'd been looking for, he pinched my leg hard enough to get my attention.

"Ow," I said, glaring at him. "What was that for?"

"Let it go for now," Max said, casually nodding at the couple sitting across from me.

"You're right," I whispered, chagrined. "Sorry. But I can't hear what they're saying."

"Probably why they're whispering, Suzy," he said with a chuckle. Then he pointed at the piece of steak still on my plate. "Are you going to finish that?"

I stared at him and frowned.

"You really haven't been paying attention, have you?"

"There's my girl," he said, removing his hand from my thigh to get back to his own dinner.

"You're so good for me, Max," I said, nuzzling his neck. "I love you so much."

"I love you too," he said, touching his fork to mine in salute. "Now eat."

I did. And kept eating for the next few minutes until Josie asked Billy Merrihew a question.

"How do you like living in New York, Billy?" she said, then slid a piece of chicken into her mouth.

"It's great," he said, almost deferring to Séance before responding.

"Expensive place to live, right?" Chef Claire said.

"You got that right," Billy said, shaking his head. "But what are you gonna do? It's where the work is. What little there is of it."

"Have you ever thought about moving to L.A.?" Josie said. "There must be a ton of acting work out there."

Séance snorted and almost spit up a mouthful of wine.

"Not an L.A. fan, huh?" Josie said, turning to the actress.

"Uh, no," Séance said. "L.A. is a total wasteland."

"I like living in L.A.," Geraldine said.

"Only because you're never there," Billy said with a shrug. "You're always on the road."

"I'm there enough to know I prefer it to the smugness of some of the New Yorkers I've met," she said, fixing a stare on Séance.

"So, you prefer the constant contact of the vacuous over sporadic conceit?" Séance said with a self-satisfied smirk I so wanted to knock off her face.

"I rest my case," Geraldine said, glancing around the table to acknowledge the laughter. "Vacuous, huh? It's nice to see you've been studying your word of the day, Séance. And you actually used it correctly in a sentence."

Séance muttered an expletive as she chewed a mouthful of salad. She grabbed her napkin and dabbed at her lips as she stared at the wall.

"Ladies, please," Billy said, glancing back and forth at them. "Let's not do this tonight, okay? Try to show a little respect for the old man."

"What have you been working on lately, Billy?" I said, doing my part to shift the conversation.

"Oh, a little of this and that," he said, shrugging. "I did a showcase for a new playwright a few months ago and got some decent reviews. But I'm paying the bills doing commercials and industrials."

"Industrials?" Chef Claire said.

"Yeah, they're corporate gigs," he said. "Usually they're short training videos on things like workplace safety or other human resource crap. They're about as exciting as watching paint dry, but they pay well. You do what you gotta do, right?"

"Sure, sure," I said before noticing Séance's scowl. "What's the matter?"

"Oh, it's nothing," she said, then continued. "But industrials are to acting what house painting is to art."

"It's called work, Séance," Billy said, giving his girlfriend a dark stare.

"I know what you call it, Billy," she snapped.

"You should cut her some slack, Billy," Geraldine said as she gave the actress an evil grin. "It shouldn't surprise you Séance isn't familiar with what actually constitutes work."

"I've had about enough of you," Séance said, returning Geraldine's stare. "And for the record, I work my butt off trying to perfect my craft."

"As long as you don't have to lower yourself to do anything you consider unworthy of your talents, right?" Geraldine said, leaning forward.

"Artists must remain vigilant about honing their skills," Séance said, taking a big gulp of her wine.

"Sure, I understand," Geraldine said. "And as long as you have someone around to pay your bills, you're able to *hone* to your heart's content."

"Wow," Josie whispered. "Nice shot."

"Yeah, it sure was," I whispered back.

"Will you two please stop?" Billy snapped loud enough to get the attention of the rest of the table. "Sorry," he said, glancing at Jim and Mary. "It's been a tough day."

"Sure, Billy," Jim said, glancing back and forth at Geraldine and Séance. "Don't worry about it. No problem."

"All of a sudden, I feel a migraine coming on," Séance said, getting to her feet. "I'm going to head back to the hotel and lie down."

"I'll drive you," Billy said, starting to get up.

"No, you stay," Séance said. "I feel like walking." Then she glared at Geraldine again. "It's something we New Yorkers do. Unlike the people in L.A. who drive to their next-door neighbor's house."

"Since you're leaving, Séance," Geraldine said with an evil grin. "I'm gonna give you that one. I know how important it is for you to have the last word."

Séance flashed a brief glare at Geraldine then thanked Jim and Mary, said her goodbyes and made a dramatic exit. Billy settled back into his seat and looked at his sister.

"What's the matter with you, Geraldine?"

"Me? I'm not the one living with Princess Parasite."

"No, you're not," Billy said. "But I am."

"And whose fault is that?" Geraldine said. "But don't worry, Billy. I'm sure the situation will resolve itself soon enough. As soon as Séance finds someone who has a bit more money and is willing to tolerate her crap, she'll be out of the roach-box you call an apartment faster than you can take a curtain call."

"You don't know what you're talking about," Billy said, pushing his plate away.

"Get rid of her, Billy. She's bad news," Geraldine said. "Come to L.A. and live with me. I've got tons of room, and I'm hardly ever there."

"Séance would never agree to live in L.A.," Billy said.

"Perfect," Geraldine said. "Because she's not invited."

"This is not the time to have this conversation," he said, taking a sip of wine. "In fact, I'd rather not have this conversation again."

"Because you know I'm right," Geraldine said.

They both sat back in their chairs, and an uncomfortable silence filled our end of the table. But the loud voices coming from the other end of the table soon made up for it. We all glanced down the table when Charlie's two brothers were voicing their displeasure and appeared to be on the verge of yelling. It didn't look like they were arguing with each other. Rather, it appeared the topic of conversation was the cause of their anger.

"What are you talking about?" one of the brothers, a burly man by the name of Phil, said as he stared at Mary in disbelief.

"Why does that surprise you?" Mary said calmly.

"A reverse mortgage?" Phil said. "Why the hell did he do something so stupid?"

"So he had enough to live on," Mary said. "And it was his house. Quite frankly, I don't see how it's any of your business, Uncle Phil."

"None of my business?" Phil said, his voice rising another notch.

"No, it's not," Jim said, shaking his head. "The house was pretty much all Charlie had. Why shouldn't he take out some of the equity so he could live comfortably?"

"It was your idea, wasn't it?" the other brother, an overweight, bald man named Wilbur, snapped at Mary.

Mary shrugged.

"We discussed it with him before he did it," she said. "He wanted our opinion and Jim and I thought it made a ton of sense. The house had been paid off for years. Why shouldn't he use some of the equity?"

"Because he should have left...," Phil said before trailing off.

"Typical Charlie," Wilbur said. "Only thinking of himself."

"Here we go," Billy whispered.

"It was his house," Charlie's sister said. Shirley was a small woman with a squeaky voice, and she had her hands folded in front of her on the table. "And he didn't owe us anything."

"Nobody asked for your opinion, Shirley," Wilbur said, waving her off with the back of his hand.

"No one ever does," Shirley said without emotion.

"That should tell you all you need to know," Wilbur said, not even bothering to make eye contact with her. He focused a hard stare on Mary. "How much equity did he manage to burn through?"

"I have no idea," she said. "It was none of my business. You know, since it was *his* money."

"I can't believe it," Phil said, tossing back the last half of his glass of wine. "Well, maybe things will sort themselves out when we get a chance to take a look at the will."

Mary and Jim glanced at each other before she responded.

"That might be a problem. It appears Uncle Charlie didn't leave a will."

"What?" Phil said, stunned. "He couldn't pull himself away from the computer long enough to write down how his crap was going to be distributed?"

"Maybe he didn't feel the need to write it down," Jim said with a casual shrug.

"What's that supposed to mean?" Wilbur said.

"Without a will, my guess is everything will go to Billy and Geraldine," Jim said.

"Unbelievable," Phil said, glancing down the table. "They don't need the money. At least the Graverobber doesn't. And the *actor* has been living in poverty so long, he's probably used to it by now."

"Yeah," Wilbur said, nodding in agreement with his brother. "He wears the starving artist label like a badge of honor."

"Enough. Stop. Both of you," Shirley said calmly. "Leave the kids out of it. I'm sure Charlie had his reasons."

"I can't believe it," Phil said. "You would think the guy could have at least tossed a few bones in our direction."

"I'm so sorry you have to hear this," Geraldine whispered.

"Don't worry about it," I said, rubbing my forehead as my neurons began firing. "Did you guys know he didn't have a will?"

"I'd barely spoken with him the past fifteen years," Billy said, shaking his head. He glanced at Geraldine. "Did you know?"

"No, Dad wouldn't have ever shared that with me," Geraldine said. "And between all of us at this end of the table, there's no way he would have left a nickel to either one of those vultures."

"But he and Aunt Shirley always got along," Billy said. "I'd be surprised if he didn't leave something to her."

"Yeah, me too," Geraldine said.

"What about all his memorabilia?" I said.

"What about it?" she said.

"Is it worth anything?"

"I doubt if there was anything really valuable," she said. "He had a fascination for World War two artifacts, but I'm sure most of it was junk."

"Well, there's a lot of it," Josie said. "There must be a dozen boxes at the house."

"At least," Chef Claire said. "What do you want us to do with it?"

Geraldine and Billy looked at each other for several moments.

"I guess we should stop by the house and go through it," Billy said with a shrug.

"It would be great if you could do that, Billy," his sister said.

"Oh, no," he said, giving Geraldine a small smile. "You're gonna help. You're the memorabilia expert in the family."

Geraldine thought about it then eventually nodded.

"Okay," she said. "Would it be all right if we stopped by the house tomorrow?"

"I don't see why not," Chef Claire said, then glanced at Josie for her agreement. Josie nodded immediately. "Swing by in the morning. I'll cook breakfast."

"What are you gonna make?" Josie said, giving Chef Claire her undivided attention.

"Does it matter?" Chef Claire said.

"It never has before."

Chapter 6

"Try not to do anything stupid while you guys are in New York," I said, giving Max a hug and a kiss.

"You mean like getting my face stuck to an ice bar?" he said with a grin.

"I thought we agreed not to talk about it," I said, gently punching him on the arm.

Our recent pre-wedding girls' trip to Vegas continued to be a topic of conversation around town. Several mishaps I had gotten caught up in were regularly retold, and I subconsciously rubbed the side of my face where a freezer burn had developed after I had inadvertently fallen asleep on top of an ice bar while stuck inside a freezer posing as a high-end, vodka tasting room. Several other things had happened while we were in Sin City, but for some reason, getting my face getting stuck to the ice always produced the biggest laugh.

"Oh, there's my ride," Max said, glancing out the kitchen window. "We're going to leave Paulie's car at the airstrip. It shouldn't be a problem, right?"

"It should be fine," I said. "You're only going to be gone one night. What's the final count of guys who are coming to New York?"

Max did the math in his head.

"Fifteen, I think," he said. "They're flying in from all over then heading up here for the wedding."

"I can't wait to meet them," I said, giving him a kiss on the cheek. "Have a good time."

"You too," he said, then gave me a quizzical look. "And try not to obsess over what happened to Charlie. I don't want you stressed out at the wedding."

"Oh, don't worry," I said, laughing. "I'm plenty stressed out without worrying about Charlie. Now go. Paulie and Rooster are waiting." I glanced out the window. "Is that Jackson and Freddie in the backseat?"

"It is," Max said. "Jackson managed to figure out a way to get a couple days off from the store."

"Great. He hasn't had a day off in months."

"And Freddie's still beating himself up about missing what happened to Charlie," Max said. "I finally convinced him a Yankees game and a night on the town in New York would take his mind off his troubles."

He gave me another hug and kiss then knelt down to stroke Chloe's head who had been on point all morning since she'd figured out somebody was about to be on the move.

"You take good care of your Mama, Chloe," Max said, then stood and leaned in for a peck on the cheek before tossing a garment bag over his shoulder. "I'll give you a call as soon as we get in."

"Have fun. Love you," I said, opening the door for him. "No, Chloe. You're staying here with me."

"Love you too," he said with a wave on his way out.

I watched him head down the driveway and waited until Paulie drove off with a soft tap on the horn. I headed for the living room and stretched out on a couch. Chloe waited until I got comfortable then joined me. Josie entered from her bedroom moments later rubbing her eyes and trailed by Captain.

"I heard a car horn," she said, yawning. "Did Max leave?"

"He did," I said as Chloe flipped over onto her back for a morning tummy rub. Captain approached and waited for me to say hello to him. Then he nudged Chloe with a wet nose and wagged his tail as he waited for her to respond. "How did you sleep?"

"Apart from dealing with the bed hog over there, I slept fine," Josie said in mock indignance. "Yes, I'm talking about you."

Captain woofed at her and headed for the back door. Chloe followed, as did Al and Dente as soon as they emerged from the hallway. Chef Claire entered the living room and managed a sleepy nod.

"Coffee's already made," I said, sitting up on the couch. "You want me to let the beasts out for their morning pee?"

"No, I've got it," Chef Claire said, heading for the kitchen. "Josie, you want coffee?"

"Yes, please," Josie said, plopping down in one of the overstuffed chairs. "Did you sleep or were you up all night pondering the possibilities?"

"The possibilities of who might have killed Charlie?"

"Yeah."

"So you saw it too?" I said.

"It was a little hard to miss," she said, shaking her head. "What a group, huh?"

"I guess you can't blame Geraldine and Billy for getting out of town and staying away," I said. "Charlie had his moments, but his brothers are off the planet. Where on earth did they get the idea Charlie should be leaving money to them in his will?"

"I have no idea," Josie said. "I'm still trying to sort out the dynamics between Geraldine and Séance."

"Definitely no love lost there."

"No, love lost where?" Chef Claire said, coming back into the living room carrying two mugs of coffee. She handed one to Josie and sat down. She took a sip and nodded. "It's good. Well done," she said, raising her mug to me in salute.

"Geraldine and Séance," Josie said. "When I was talking to her before dinner, Geraldine said she recently visited the happy couple in New York."

"You think she's right about Séance only hanging around until she finds a better option?" I said.

"I do," Josie said.

"Me too," Chef Claire said. "She's too self-absorbed to be any other way. You know, always looking out for number one. And in case I was going too fast for you, Séance is the number one in question."

"Got it," I said, making a face at Chef Claire. "Geraldine seems very protective of Billy. I don't remember her ever being like that when we were kids."

"She's probably mellowing with age," Josie said. "Or they've realized they're all each other has when it comes to family."

"Maybe," I said. "And her offer for Billy to come and live with her in L.A. seems genuine."

"But not while Séance is leading him around by the nose," Josie said.

"Yeah, Geraldine made it pretty clear," Chef Claire said. "Those two are toxic with each other."

"My guess is Séance has the same effect on most people," Josie said. "I don't like her."

"Now, there's a shock," I said, laughing.

"How does Geraldine compare to the way she was when you guys were kids?" Chef Claire said, tucking her legs underneath her on the couch.

"She seems a lot more confident," I said. "But she's more guarded. You know, she'll divulge some things but deflect if the conversation gets too personal. Maybe she gets it from her dad."

"Money will do that," Josie said.

"You think she's making a lot of money?" I said.

"According to her, she's doing well," Josie said. "Apparently, rare antiquities are big business if you have connections with the right folks."

"The right folks being rich people interested in getting their hands on one-of-a-kind antiquities?" I said.

"Nothing gets past you," Josie said, saluting me with her mug. "I get people wanting to buy the stuff, but how the heck does she find the people willing to sell it?"

"Charlie seemed to be able to do it," I said.

"Yeah, but from what Charlie told us he dealt with the sort of stuff you find on eBay," Josie said. "Geraldine deals with truly rare collectibles. Unique and very expensive. And it sounded like the last thing her clients want is publicity."

"You think she deals with the black market?" I said.

"I think Geraldine is willing to deal with whatever she needs to," Josie said. "She was talking about some chair she managed to track down in Europe. The chair sold for a million and a half."

"For one chair?" I said.

"Yeah. It was a loveseat that belonged to Napoleon and Josephine," Josie said.

"Really?" I said. "How did Geraldine manage to find it?"

"She wouldn't say," Josie said, sipping her coffee. "She called it proprietary information."

"Shouldn't a chair like that be in a French museum?" Chef Claire said.

"Apparently, the French government thought the same thing," Josie said. "Hence, Geraldine's reluctance to reveal her source."

"Did she tell you who bought it?" I said.

"Some tech billionaire out west," Josie said. "Geraldine said she made a quarter million on the deal."

"Geez," Chef Claire said, laughing. "A long way from IKEA."

"Well, the chair came assembled, so…," Josie deadpanned.

Chef Claire and I laughed. Then Chef Claire got up and glanced at Josie.

"I'm going to let the bruisers in," she said. "You want a refill?"

"Yes, please," Josie said, handing her the mug. Then she glanced over at me. "What's your take on it so far?"

"I don't have a clue," I said. "But the reaction both brothers had last night was definitely off the charts. And the only other anger I noticed was between Geraldine and Séance."

"Yeah, I don't get it either," Josie said. "And from what we heard, Charlie didn't have enough money for anybody to kill him over."

"The lack of a will seems strange," I said. "Charlie always seemed to have his act together. And since he was so independent, it seems odd he would leave his affairs open to any sort of debate after he was gone."

"I thought the same thing," Josie said, sitting up in her chair as the four dogs trotted into the living room. She made room for Captain who hopped up on her lap, causing her to momentarily disappear from sight. "Maybe it *was* an accident."

"I'd like to think so," I said, groaning when Chloe draped herself over my lap. I scratched her ears as I shook my head. "I have my doubts. But I can't come up with any sort of motive."

"Then I guess you'll have to put it out of your mind and focus on the wedding," she said, accepting the fresh mug of coffee Chef Claire was holding out. "Did you decide what we're having for breakfast?"

"How does French toast sound?" Chef Claire said, sitting back down.

"With?" Josie said, raising an eyebrow.

"Probably with way too much bacon and sausage," Chef Claire said. "Since the kitchen at the new house is still a mess, I thought I'd cook here and carry it down."

"Good plan," Josie said. "What time did you tell Billy and Geraldine to swing by?"

"Nine," Chef Claire said. "Given the number of boxes, I thought we should get an early start. We have to be at your mom's no later than four to help her get ready for the party."

"Ah, yes," I said. "The *penultimate* pre-wedding party. Her words, not mine."

"This one is casual, right?" Josie said.

"It is," I said. "And it's open to anybody from town who wants to stop by."

"That was nice of her to do," Chef Claire said.

"Yeah, it was," I said. "She wanted to have at least one event where everybody could kick back and relax before the main event. I think I'll invite the Merrihew clan."

"Here we go," Josie said, laughing as she glanced over at Chef Claire.

"What?" I said in mock protest. "They'll get a chance to catch up with some folks they haven't seen in a long time."

"Whatever you say," Josie said, getting to her feet. "C'mon, Chef Claire. I'll give you a hand making breakfast. Let's give Columbo a chance to develop her game plan."

"I wouldn't actually call it a game plan," I said to myself as I stretched back out on the couch. "It's barely a notion."

I glanced around at all four dogs who had their heads cocked at me. Then they heard the unmistakable sound of the fridge opening and made a beeline for the kitchen.

Deciding I would play it by ear until some options opened up, I closed my eyes and dozed off until the smell of bacon and French toast woke me with a start.

Chapter 7

Josie set her knife and fork down on the plate then pushed it away. She groaned and pressed a hand against her stomach. She did her best to ignore the looks we were giving her, but she eventually succumbed to our intense stares.

"What?" she said, stifling a burp.

"I told you to slow down," Chef Claire said, then frowned at her. "Geez, Josie, how the heck did you manage to get syrup in your hair?"

"It's a mystery," she said, grabbing a strand of hair to examine it for signs of damage. "Whew. I'm stuffed. "Fantastic, Chef Claire. Thank you."

Josie got to her feet and groaned again.

"I'd love to stay and watch them go through a dozen boxes of junk, but I have a ten o'clock spaying. And I think I might go for a walk around the block to work this breakfast off."

"Let's hope it's a big block," I said.

"Funny," she said, kneeling down to stroke Captain's head. "You want to go for a walk or would you like to stay here with your buds?"

Captain cocked his head and actually appeared to be giving the question some serious thought. Then he sniffed the air and stared up lovingly at the stack of bacon piled high on a plate.

Josie laughed then gave the Newfie a gentle thump on the side and got to her feet.

"I've been cast aside for the prospect of bacon," she said. "Thanks a lot, Captain."

"He gets it from his mother," I deadpanned.

"You're on fire today."

There was a knock on the door and Josie headed for the front door. Moments later, Geraldine, trailed closely by Billy and Séance, entered the kitchen.

"Is she okay?" Billy said, nodding at the departing Josie.

"She'll be fine," Chef Claire said. "It's merely a self-inflicted carbohydrate wound."

"I hate carbohydrates," Séance said with a frown.

"Now there's a surprise," I whispered before sliding a piece of French toast into my mouth.

"Then breakfast might be a problem," Chef Claire said, doing her best to remain diplomatic. "Do you like bacon?"

"Bacon?" Séance said as if Chef Claire had asked her to donate a lung to science. "No, I'm sorry. I don't eat *ba-con*."

"I think we have some fruit in the fridge," Chef Claire said, opening the refrigerator. "Since we haven't moved in yet, we're still a bit short on supplies. How does a bowl of cantaloupe and watermelon sound?"

"That would be fine," Séance said.

"The life of a working actress, right?" Billy said, doing his best to diffuse the tension. "Constantly counting calories. You know, since the camera adds ten pounds."

"I've already gained two pounds on this field trip," Séance snapped at Billy as if it were somehow his fault. "I hate being out of my routine."

All four dogs sat nearby with their heads cocked trying to make sense of the whiny interloper. Chloe, sensing my discomfort, emitted a low, guttural growl. It immediately got the actress's attention.

"Does that thing bite?" Séance said, nodding at my Aussie shepherd.

"Not unless I tell her to," I said, beaming at her. "And she's not a thing. Her name is Chloe."

"I've never been much of a dog person," Séance said, flinching when she got her first good look at Captain. "How about him? The one that looks like a bear cub. Is he dangerous?"

"No, he's a big baby," I said, leaning down to stroke the Newfie's head. "Aren't you, Captain?"

Captain woofed softly once but didn't take his eyes off the actress.

"Go ahead, pet him," I said.

"Not gonna happen," Séance said, spearing a piece of watermelon and delicately sliding it into her mouth. "Good fruit. Almost as good as what we get in the City."

63

"Yeah, I know," I said, glancing at Chef Claire. "But it's hard to compete with New York. You know, what with it being the fruit growing mecca it is."

Séance gave me a sideways glance but decided to let my snarky comment pass without comment. Chef Claire gestured for them to sit down and placed plates in front of Billy and Geraldine. They both started eating as they glanced around the kitchen.

"This brings back some memories, huh?" Billy said to his sister.

"It sure does," Geraldine said. "This is fantastic, Chef Claire. Thank you."

"You're very welcome. I almost forgot you guys grew up in this house. When was the last time you were here?"

"Well, let's see," Geraldine said. "I haven't been here since Dad's eightieth birthday. What's that, geez, twelve years? Wow. Long time."

"It's even longer for me," Billy said. "About twenty years ago, Dad and I decided our rare conversations were best handled over the phone. It was one of the few things we actually agreed on."

"That's so sad," Chef Claire said, getting to her feet. "I'll be right back." She started to exit the kitchen but stopped when her Goldens started to follow her. "No, you guys stay here. I'm going to the bathroom to wash the dog off me. Your tagging along won't make it any easier."

She knelt down and gave both dogs a long hug then headed off. I watched Billy and Geraldine as they continued to glance around and let childhood memories wash over them. Séance quickly worked her way through her bowl of fruit then her face flushed red when I caught her giving Billy's plate a loving stare. She quickly recovered and got to her feet.

"I think I might have a bit more fruit," she announced.

"Help yourself," I said, deciding to have some fun with her. "Are you sure you wouldn't like some French toast and bacon?"

"I'm positive. But I need to use the bathroom first."

"Chef Claire will be out in a minute," I said.

"No, it can't wait," Séance said. "I'll use the one upstairs."

She gave the dogs a wide berth as she walked past them and all four trailed close behind to keep an eye on her.

"The boxes are all in the living room," I said, glancing back and forth at the two siblings.

"Yes, we saw them on our way in," Billy said. "I can't believe how much crap Dad bought over the years."

"Every time we spoke on the phone he always spent the first ten minutes telling me about his latest acquisition," Geraldine said, shaking her head. "He was convinced it was going to *knock my socks off*."

"Your dad thought he could find something you might be able to sell for him?" I said.

"It was always hard to tell what he wanted," Geraldine said, tearing up. "I think he was jealous of how I'd made a successful career out of what was basically a hobby for him."

"Jealous sounds a bit harsh," I said.

"Yeah, I know," she said, exhaling softly. "But our relationship was…complicated. To say the least."

"At least you had a relationship with him," Billy said, polishing off the last of his breakfast.

"Let's not go there today, okay, Billy?" Geraldine said.

Chef Claire returned and knelt down to greet all four dogs. Soon they had her pinned on the floor, giving her kisses, their tails wagging furiously.

"So much for washing off," she said, climbing to her feet and topping off everyone's coffee.

"Have you given any more thought to my offer?" Geraldine said to her brother.

"About moving to L.A.?"

"Yeah," Geraldine said, taking a sip.

"I can't," Billy said. "Séance is adamant about not leaving New York."

"Sounds perfect," Geraldine said. "Three thousand miles would be a great buffer zone."

"Don't start," Billy said, making solid eye contact with her. "You don't know anything about our relationship." He looked away then nodded. "We're rock solid. And I think things are about to turn around for her."

"Billy, from what I've heard, nobody can stand working with her," Geraldine said. "And how old is she now?"

"She's about to turn thirty-four," Billy said. "But do me a favor and don't mention age when she's around. It's kind of a sore point."

"If it hasn't happened for her in New York by now, for either one of you, chances are it won't," she said, placing a hand on her brother's arm. "But you could get a ton of TV work. And I've got some clients who could help you out."

"So, what's stopping you?" Billy said, forcing a laugh.

"The presence of the Wicked Witch of the North. What else do you think is stopping me?"

"You're saying you're unwilling to help me out because Séance is in my life?"

"I've always been willing to help you, Billy," Geraldine said, glaring at her brother.

"You're right," he said, chagrined. "Sorry."

"She's a user, Billy. Trust me, I've met a million of them in L.A. Normally, they don't bother me. You get used to it. It's kinda like the weather out there. But, unfortunately, this user is doing it to my brother."

"I know what I'm doing, Geraldine."

"Maybe we should head into the living room and leave you two alone," I said, starting to get up.

"No, don't worry about it," Geraldine said. "I think we're done. I'm all talked out."

We all flinched when he heard a blood-curdling scream coming from upstairs. All four dogs scrambled to their feet and bolted for the stairs. We followed in close pursuit. Séance was standing in the hallway directly below the section of the ceiling that contained the collapsible ladder leading up to the attic. She was shaking, and her expression was a mixture of anger and fear.

"What on earth is the matter?" Billy said, attempting to drape an arm over her shoulder she immediately shook off.

"That," she said, pointing at a stain on the floor. "I almost stepped in it."

"Stepped in what?" Geraldine said, staring down at the floor.

"In dried blood," Séance said. "It's disgusting."

"I'm so sorry, Séance," Chef Claire said, leading her by the arm away from the bloodstain. "Josie and I tried to get it all out of the wood, but some of it soaked in. We need to have this section sanded down then varnished."

"Well, I should certainly hope so," Séance said, then softened. "That's where you found the body?"

"Yes," Chef Claire said.

"I can't believe I almost stepped on a dead guy," Séance said, her eyes wild.

"Uh, not to nitpick, but-" I said.

"Let it go," Chef Claire said, squeezing my forearm.

"Oh, no," Séance said, massaging her temples.

"What's the matter?" Billy said.

"I feel another migraine coming on," the actress said. "I need to lie down."

"Feel free to use one of the bedrooms," Chef Claire said.

"Not a chance," Séance said. "Billy, would you mind giving me a ride back to the hotel?"

"Sure, Sweetie," he said, taking her by the hand and leading her down the stairs. "I'll be right back, Geraldine."

"Take your time," she said, then beamed at Séance. "I do hope you feel better soon."

"Yeah, I bet you do," Séance said as she headed down the stairs.

We followed them down the stairs, and the dogs eventually settled on a large rug in the living room, apparently worn out from all the excitement.

"She's something else," I said to no one in particular as I watched them drive away. "And very fragile."

"Yeah, almost birdlike," Chef Claire said.

"Good description," I said, nodding. "What sort of bird does she remind you of?"

"I'm not exactly sure," Chef Claire said, then muttered under her breath. "Maybe a vulture."

"Well, whatever species it is, let's hope there's an open season on it." Geraldine shook her head then clapped her hands once. "Okay, let's go look at some boxes of crap."

Chapter 8

A half-hour later, the living room resembled a war-memorabilia garage sale, sans the garage. Whatever skills Charlie lacked in his ability to identify and procure artifacts of value, he more than made up for it in volume. Dozens of World War II helmets, ration kits, uniforms and assorted clothing, pistols and bayonets, along with a host of other items I didn't recognize were strewn across the floor. But Geraldine, using her skills as an expert in the field of collectibles, had organized the items into what appeared to be logical groups.

When the final box was unpacked, she and Billy sat down on the floor with their legs splayed and their backs against the wall staring in disbelief at the collection surrounding them.

"I can't believe it," Geraldine said, shaking her head.

"This is the sum total of his life?" Billy said, picking up one of the pistols and examining it.

"It certainly appears to be the case," she said, taking a long pull from a bottle of water.

"What do we do with it?" he said, accepting the bottle from her.

"First, we need to box it up," she said. "We can't leave the place looking like this."

"Take your time," Chef Claire said. "Josie and I aren't moving in until after the wedding."

They both glanced up to nod their thanks then resumed casting their eyes over the collection.

"Is this stuff worth anything?" Billy said.

"Yeah, some of it," Geraldine said, nodding at the collection of pistols. "Those German Lugers will fetch some decent money. And I think some of the silverware might be rare. But I'll have to get my appraiser to take a close look at it. The rest of it you can probably unload at one of the costume places supplying the film industry. They're always looking for inventory from that period."

"You said *I* might be able to unload it," Billy said, glancing over at his sister.

"Yeah, I'll help you get rid of it," she said. "But the money is all yours. Including whatever equity in the house Dad didn't burn through."

"I'm not comfortable with that, Geraldine," he said. "Half of it is yours."

"Don't want it, don't need it," she said, climbing to her feet but continuing to lean against the wall.

"No, it's not right."

"Take the money, Billy," she said. "Consider it his penance for all the crap he put you through."

"But it's the last thing he would have wanted," Billy said.

"I know. All the more reason to take it."

71

Billy emitted a sad chuckle and stared off at the far wall.

"Unbelievable," Geraldine said, taking another look around the room. "Geez, why didn't he just take up golf?"

"Yeah," Billy said softly. "But he was never big on fresh air. Said it always gave him a headache. You know what's really strange?"

"What?"

"There's no inventory," he said. "Dad was always meticulous about writing things down and keeping records."

"You're right," Geraldine said, glancing at Chef Claire. "You didn't happen to come across anything, did you?"

"No," Chef Claire said, shaking her head. "We've been through the entire downstairs, including your dad's office. I can check with Josie, but I don't think we did."

"Check with Josie about what?" Josie said, opening the screen door.

"How was your walk?" I said.

"It was great. It's a beautiful morning. We should be out on the River."

"Maybe we'll have a bit of time tomorrow," I said.

Josie noticed the floor strewn with artifacts and frowned.

"Did we declare war on somebody while I was out?"

"We were wondering if you came across any sort of inventory for this stuff," Chef Claire said.

"Nope, I didn't see anything," she said, kneeling down to pet all four dogs who had managed to tip-toe their way across the crowded floor. "I stopped by on my way back to the Inn. I thought I'd take the bruisers off your hands."

"Probably a good idea," I said. "This is an accident waiting to happen."

"Okay, I'll see you in a bit," she said, then turned to Billy and Geraldine. "You guys coming to the party tonight?"

"I think we will," Billy said. "And thanks for the invite."

"It should be fun," Josie said. "C'mon guys. You ready to head to the Inn?"

All four dogs headed straight out the door and stood on the porch with their tails wagging furiously.

"My work is done," she said, laughing as she watched the dogs. "See you guys later."

"Okay, Billy," Geraldine said, grabbing an empty box. "Let's start packing this crap up. I'll have it shipped to L.A. and get the appraisal done. Then I'll get the word out it's available and we'll see what happens."

"You want some money to help out with the shipping and appraisal?"

"Don't worry about it," she said. "Let's box it up the way it's organized on the floor."

"Got it," Billy said. "What do you think it's worth?"

"All in?" Geraldine said, placing her hands on her hips as she took another look around the room. "Hard to say. My best guess is somewhere around twenty, maybe twenty-five thousand. If you're lucky."

"I wonder what he paid for all this stuff?"

"Knowing Dad, probably a lot more than what it's worth."

Chapter 9

Josie grabbed a handful of bite-sized then tossed the bag to me. I slid it back into the desk drawer and closed it tight. I caught the look all four dogs were giving me and folded like a lawn chair.

"I suppose you guys want a cookie?" I said as I reached for the jar of treats sitting on my desk. I tossed one each to all of them, and they expertly snatched their cookie out of the air and quickly munched through them. "Why don't you head outside and get some fresh air?"

"What a good idea," Josie said, getting up off the couch to open the office door. "Go play."

All four dogs trotted out the door and made an immediate left. Moments later, I glanced out the window and watched as they said hello to several of our permanent guests. Captain and Al spotted the rope toy at the same time and began a furious game of tuggy that ended, as it always did, with Captain victorious.

"What are they doing?" Josie said, sprawling back out on the couch.

"Living large," I said, laughing as I put my feet up on my desk. "You feel like going through some paperwork?"

"Can it wait?"

"It can."

"Good," she said, yawning. "Is Chef Claire still over at the house?"

"Yeah," I said. "Billy and Geraldine finally got all the boxes packed up and loaded. They headed to the post office to ship them to Geraldine's place in L.A. Chef Claire stayed behind to do some more work in the kitchen."

"She's relentless."

"You know how she likes to be settled," I said, gently rocking in my chair.

"Reminds me of someone else I know."

"Hey, I'm doing pretty good," I said in mock protest. "I haven't cried in two days."

Josie laughed, fell silent and stared off at the wall.

"You're worried about seeing Summerman, aren't you?" I said, treading carefully around what I knew was a very sensitive subject.

"I wouldn't say I'm worried," she said, glancing over at me. "But to be honest, I wish I didn't have to deal with him. It's going to be awkward, to say the least."

Summerman and Josie had been an item a few years ago, and their relationship had burned hot before fizzling out completely. At a minimum, I knew she was curious about seeing him again, but I also knew her decision to no longer be with him was resolute. The fact his band was playing at the wedding reception nagged at her, but she would never say or do anything to put a damper on my wedding day.

"Thank you," I said softly.

"For what?"

"For dealing with him playing at the reception as well as you are," I said, shrugging. "Most people would probably make a big deal about having to spend a whole day around her ex-boyfriend."

"You're making too much of it, Suzy. And I won't be spending the whole day around him. We're both going to be busy."

"Still, I want you to know how much I appreciate it," I said.

"Consider it a wedding gift," she deadpanned.

"That's all I'm getting?" I said, laughing.

"It was either that or a toaster oven," she said, resting her head on the end of the couch and closing her eyes. "And by midnight, he and his band will be on their buses heading to the next show."

My mother tapped softly on the office door and poked her head in. Josie sat up and made room for her to sit down.

"Hi, Mom," I said, getting up to give her a hug.

"Hello, darling. Josie, you're looking very relaxed."

"I'm trying to catch my breath," Josie said. "I've got three annual exams and another surgery scheduled for this afternoon. How are you doing, Mrs. C.?"

"Wonderful," my mother said. "Everything is right on schedule and going off without a hitch."

"It ought to," I said, laughing. "I don't think the military does as much planning going to war as you have with this wedding."

"It's all about the details, darling. I ran into Billy and Geraldine Merrihew at the post office."

"Yeah, they spent the morning at the house going through Charlie's memorabilia," Josie said.

"I invited them and the rest of the family to the party," I said.

"Good," she said. "It's been ages since I've seen a lot of those folks."

"What time do you need us over there?" I said.

"That's why I stopped by," my mother said. "Actually, I'm not going to need your help at all. Everything is ready to go. All I need to do is make sure the caterers and bartenders know the drill. Stop by any time after six. Have the boys landed in New York yet?"

"Max texted me about an hour ago," I said. "As soon as they got off the plane they headed straight for the stadium. The Yankees are playing this afternoon."

"But they will be back tomorrow in time for the rehearsal dinner, right?" my mother said.

"I'm sure they will," I said, grinning at her. "I doubt very much if either one wants to suffer the consequences if they aren't."

"You got that right," she said, nodding.

My phone buzzed, and I checked the number. I didn't recognize it and thought about letting it go to voicemail but changed my mind and answered.

"This is Suzy."

"Hey, Suzy. It's Summerman."

"Hey, Summerman," I said, immediately putting the phone on speaker. "We were just talking about you."

"Probably not as much as you will be after this phone call," he said solemnly. "We've got a problem."

"What sort of problem?" my mother said with a deep scowl as she leaned forward.

"Oh, hi, Mrs. C.," Summerman said. "How are you doing?"

"I'll let you know in a minute," she said. "What's going on?"

"Well, this is really hard to tell you, but we aren't going to be able to make the wedding," he said softly.

"Is this some sort of joke, Summerman?" my mother said, then looked at me. "Did you put him up to this, darling? You know, to see if you could give me a heart attack before the wedding?"

"I swear, Mom. I have no idea what he's talking about."

"What about you, Josie?" my mother said, wheeling around to face her. "I know how you love your practical jokes."

"Don't look at me," Josie said, shaking her head.

"Oh, Josie's there," Summerman said. "Hi, Josie."

"Summerman," Josie said without emotion.

"What's going on, Summerman?" my mother said.

"Well, the short version is we had a bit of a problem going through immigration today."

"Immigration?" I said. "Where are you?"

"Riyadh," Summerman said.

"What on earth are you doing in Saudi Arabia?" my mother said, sliding into a chair next to my desk and staring hard at the phone.

"We played a private party here last night for one of the Saudi princes."

"Keep talking, Summerman," my mother said. "I'm about to have a stroke here."

"Yeah, I'm sure you are, Mrs. C.," he said. "And I am incredibly sorry to have to do this."

"What happened?" I said.

"We did a show a couple of nights ago in Morocco. And one of our horn players thought it would be a good idea to buy some *local product* while we were there."

"Local product?" I said. "I take it we aren't talking about tapestries."

"Unfortunately, no," Summerman said. "He bought some Moroccan hash while we were in town."

"And he got caught with it at Saudi immigration?" my mother said.

"He did. It was in his carry-on bag," he said. "The idiot forgot it was there."

"How the heck did he forget?" I said.

"He'd been smoking some of it right before the flight."

"Got it," I said, rubbing my forehead as I kept a close eye on my mother. "How much did he get caught with?"

"Eight ounces."

"He got caught with a half-pound of hash by the Saudis?" I said, stunned.

"Well, look at you," Josie deadpanned. "Doing fractions in your head."

"Shut it," I said, then focused on the phone. "I assume he got arrested."

"He did," Summerman said. "And it's going to take us a couple of days to get it sorted out. If we can."

"Can't you pay some sort of fine?" my mother said.

"It's a bit different over here when it comes to drugs, Mrs. C. And since he got caught with eight ounces, they're talking about charging him with intent to sell."

"Was he planning on selling it?" I said.

"No way," Summerman said, managing a small laugh. "Scotty doesn't even like sharing with the rest of the band."

"I hear their drug laws are pretty draconian," I said. "What sort of jail time is he looking at?"

"Jail time? Scotty should be so lucky," Summerman said. "If he gets convicted of being a drug dealer, he could be looking at the death penalty."

"What?" I said, stunned.

"Yeah. Now you see why we won't be able to leave until we get this sorted out. The best case is a couple of days. Assuming I can call in a few favors with Prince Abdul and hope he's able to work his magic."

"I'm sorry he's going through that, Summerman," my mother said.

I was impressed. I had expected her to start climbing the walls as soon as she'd heard the news.

"Yeah, it's not good," Summerman said, sounding exhausted. "Stoned and stupid is an ugly combination. I'm so sorry, guys. We were all looking forward to playing at the wedding. And I know I've really left you in the lurch."

"It's out of your control, Summerman," my mother said calmly.

"I promise I'll figure out a way to make it up to you," he said.

"Don't worry about it," my mother said. "Okay, I'm sure you have bigger problems to deal with at the moment."

"Actually, I need to run to a meeting with some folks from the embassy."

"Thanks for letting us know, Summerman," my mother said.

"Believe me, it was the least I could do. Thanks for being so understanding, Mrs. C. I really wasn't looking forward to making this phone call. And congratulations, Suzy. I hope you and Max have a wonderful day and a great honeymoon."

"Thanks, Summerman," I said softly.

"You take care of yourself, Josie," he said.

"You too, Summerman."

I ended the call and leaned forward with my elbows on the desk.

"Bummer," I said. "Geez, the death penalty. I sure hope it's good hash."

"Indeed," my mother said.

"You're remarkably calm, Mom," I said. "I'm impressed."

"There's nothing anybody can do about it," she said with a shrug. "Fortunately, I have a backup plan."

"You do? Well, that's great, Mom."

"Maybe you won't be making fun of my tendency to overplan the next time," she said, raising an eyebrow at me.

"So, what's your backup plan?"

"I'm going to call Reggie," she said, getting to her feet.

I sat upright in my chair and beamed at her.

"It's brilliant, Mom."

"Thank you, darling," she said, heading for the door. "I'll give you an update tonight when I see you at the party."

She gave us an over-the-shoulder wave and gently closed the door behind her.

"You really think she had a backup?" Josie said.

"Yeah, I do," I said, nodding.

We heard a knock on the door, but it stayed closed.

"Come on in," I said.

Geraldine entered and waved to both of us.

"Your mom is on a mission," she said, shaking her head. "She almost ran over me in the parking lot. Is she okay?"

"She's fine," I said. "How are you doing?"

"I'm okay," she said, sitting down. "But I couldn't remember what time the party started tonight, so I thought I'd swing by."

"Anytime after six is fine," I said. "Did you get everything shipped off?"

"We did," she said.

My phone beeped softly. I held up a hand.

"Sorry, hang on a sec. Max said he was going to text me from the game."

"Oh, I almost forgot," Geraldine said. "Yankees-Blue Jays are playing this afternoon."

"He's wondering if we have the game on," I said, reading the message.

Josie grabbed the remote and found the channel. I texted Max and told him we were watching. I read his next text and frowned.

"He says to check out the first row behind home plate," I said, glancing up at the screen.

"There they are," Josie said. "How the heck did they get those seats?"

"How do you think?" I said. "My mother knows the owner."

"Of course," Josie said. "Dumb question. What's the sign Max is holding up?"

"It says I love you, Suzy," I said, texting a sweet message to him.

"Never let him go," Geraldine said with a grin as she focused on the game.

I read his next text, responded with a short reply then set my phone down on the desk.

"He said Juan Jameson is coming up and wants to watch him hit," I said.

"Me too," Josie said, leaning forward.

"I remember him being a free agent last year," I said. "Did he sign with the Yankees?"

"No, he signed with Toronto," Josie said, then glanced over at me. "For thirty million a year."

"He gets thirty million a year just because he can hit a baseball?" I said, stunned.

"No, he gets thirty million a year because he can hit a baseball very, very far," Josie said.

"You got that right," Geraldine said. "And he's gorgeous."

We watched the superstar's at-bat, then Josie and Geraldine both shook their head in disgust when he meekly waved at strike three.

"He needs to learn to lay off the outside slider," Geraldine said.

"He'll have a couple more shots before the day is over," Josie said.

Geraldine stood and stretched her back.

"I've got some errands to run, then I need to swing by the funeral home," she said. "But I'll see you guys tonight."

"Looking forward to it," I said, beaming at her.

After she left, Josie checked her watch then sprawled out on the couch.

A few minutes later, my phone buzzed again. I checked the number and answered immediately.

"Hey, what's up?"

"I found something you're going to want to see," Chef Claire said.

"Okay," I said, puzzled. "Are you still at the house?"

"I am," she said. "And I've been trying to get in touch with Billy and Geraldine, but they aren't answering their phones."

"I haven't seen Billy, but Geraldine was here. She left to run some errands and handle some funeral stuff," I said. "Do you need me to track them down?"

"No, it can probably wait," she said. "And the funeral arrangements are a lot more important than this. We'll update

86

them tonight at the party. But you're definitely going to want to see this."

"Color me intrigued," I said, laughing.

"But you might want to see if you can get in touch with Jim and Mary and ask them to stop by the house," Chef Claire said. "This definitely needs a family eye on it."

"I'll be there in five," I said, ending the call.

"What is it?" Josie said.

"She didn't say," I said. "Apparently she found something at the house. You got time to come along?"

"No, duty calls," Josie said, getting up off the couch. "I have a date with a beautiful Rottweiler who needs his booster shots."

"Zoltan?"

"The one and only," she said, laughing. "And as you know from personal experience, Zoltan does not like to get his shots."

"You need some help?"

"No, Sammy's gonna give me a hand."

"Let me guess. He drew the short straw," I said, grinning at her.

"He did. I think Jill cheated."

Chapter 10

I arrived at the same time Jim and Mary were pulling into the driveway. Luna hopped out as soon as the passenger door opened and headed my way. I knelt down to pet her then got to my feet.

"She's such a good girl," I said. "Hi, guys."

"What's going on?" Jim said. "Chef Claire said she had something we needed to see."

"I've got no idea," I said, heading for the stone path leading to the front door. "She didn't go into it over the phone."

"She said a family member needed to be here," Mary said.

"She couldn't get hold of Billy and Geraldine," I said, climbing the steps.

"Both their phones have been off all morning," Mary said.

The screen door opened and Chef Claire waved us inside. She pointed at the dining room table, and we all sat down. Luna hopped up on Mary's lap and focused her attention on the same items we were all staring at.

"What are those things?" Jim said, nodding at the thick three-ring binders sitting on the table.

"I completely forgot all about them," Chef Claire said. "When I was here the other day, the day Charlie got killed, he'd been upstairs packing his boxes. I was working in the kitchen when he poked his head in and said he had an antique set of kitchen knives I might want to have."

"I remember those knives," Mary said, nodding. "I think it's the only ones they ever used."

"That's what Charlie said," Chef Claire said. "He said he liked the idea of at least one thing remaining here after he moved out."

"Surprisingly sentimental for Charlie," Jim said with a chuckle as he rubbed Luna's head. "It wasn't something he showed very often."

"No, it wasn't," Mary said. "It was sweet of him."

"It was. Anyway, I told him I'd head upstairs later and get them from him. But before I got around to it, well, you know," Chef Claire said as she choked back the emotion. She took a few moments to compose herself then continued. "I completely forgot about the knives until later on after they had removed Charlie's body."

"Do you think one of the knives might have been used to kill him?" I said.

"Geez, Suzy," Chef Claire said, scowling at me. "Not until you mentioned it. My plan has been to use them in the kitchen. But if one of them was used to kill him, that's not gonna happen."

"Sorry," I said, shrugging. "It was just a question."

"Well, try to keep them to yourself until we know a bit more," she said, still frowning. "And I cut fruit with one of them earlier. Yuk."

"I said I was sorry," I said. "Go ahead with your story. For now, we'll assume one of those knives wasn't the murder weapon."

"After we cleaned up the mess, Josie headed back home, but I decided to stick around for a while and do a bit more work in the kitchen. Then I remembered the knives. I went upstairs to the attic to look for them and eventually found them in a drawer of an armoire. And right next to the knives were those three binders."

"Okay," Mary said, again glancing at the binders. "What's in them?"

"Well, I was in such a hurry, and it was incredibly hot and stuffy in the attic, I only flipped to the first page in the first binder. It looked like a collection of family photos, so I assumed that's what they were. I carried the knives and binders downstairs, put the knives in the kitchen then tossed the binders in the top drawer of the cabinet. And proceeded to completely forget about them."

"A lot of family photos," Jim said. "Especially for a guy who hated having his picture taken as much as Charlie did."

"Yeah, I can't remember many photos being taken around the house," Mary said. "Maybe they're from Uncle Charlie's younger days."

"The binders aren't filled with family photos," Chef Claire said. "There's a few in the front section of the first binder, but it's not what Charlie used them for. It didn't even cross my mind earlier today when Billy and Geraldine were here. But they mentioned at one point it seemed strange Charlie didn't have an inventory of all his memorabilia. About a half-hour ago, I was in the kitchen when I remembered the binders. And after I flipped through the first one, I called you."

Jim pulled the first binder closer and opened it. The rest of us stood and peered over his shoulder as he began to slowly flip through the pages.

"I remember that day," Mary said, pointing at one of the photos tucked inside a clear plastic sleeve. "I had recently bought a camera and thought I'd surprise Uncle Charlie while he was in his office."

"Well, mission accomplished," Jim said, laughing at the look on Charlie's face.

"I really startled him," Mary said, laughing along. "He was sitting at his desk opening his mail when I burst into his office and snapped the photo." She nudged her husband in the back. "Keep going."

Jim flipped through several pages of family photos. I recognized most of the people. Billy and Geraldine when they were kids were featured in several shots as were Charlie's siblings. Then the photos ended and a new section of the binder began.

"It his inventory of memorabilia," Jim said, staring at the page. "Each item has its own page."

"They're all numbered in sequence," Mary said, then read from the page. "Item 1, German army helmet. Date of acquisition, May 3, 1943. Purchase price, zero dollars."

I studied the pages as Jim began to flip back and forth through the binder. Each item was numbered, and a color photo along with a brief description was included.

"The pages have an identical layout. He must have built himself a template to use," Jim said. "I have to say he got pretty good on the computer. Item number in the top right corner, photo on the left, description underneath, then the acquisition date and purchase price." He paused to glance up at Mary. "This is the Charlie I knew."

"Yeah," Mary said. "But the ones in this binder all have a purchase price of zero. They must be the items he managed to get his hands on during the war."

"Managed to get his hands on?" Jim said with a grin. "You mean the ones he stole?"

"We don't know that," she said, gently slapping the back of her husband's head.

"You said you haven't looked at the other two binders yet?" Jim said to Chef Claire.

"No, as soon as I realized it was the inventory Billy and Geraldine were looking for earlier I made the call."

"Well, let's see what else Charlie managed to get his hands on over the years," Jim said as he reached for the second binder."

The inventory of items continued. Soon, the purchase price was filled in with various amounts.

"Item eighty-two," Jim said, pausing on a page. "Nazi serving platter." Then he flinched when he saw what Charlie had paid for it. "Six hundred bucks? For a plate?" He glanced over his shoulder at Mary and grinned at her again. "The next time I drop two hundred bucks at Home Depot, I don't want to hear a word."

Jim quickly flipped through the rest of the binder then set it aside. He pulled the last binder in front of him and tried to open the cover. But it barely budged.

"Weird," he said, frowning. "It doesn't want to open."

"Let me take a look," I said.

He slid the binder toward me, and I picked it up and turned it on its side.

"Something is inside the spine," I said, pointing at a small bulge in the back of the plastic cover. I tried to peer inside then slid my index finger down the opening. "Something's jammed in here."

"What does it feel like?" Mary said.

"I think it's some sort of cloth," I said, wedging two fingers down the opening. "Actually, it feels like a chamois. You know, like you'd use to wash your car."

"You want some help?" Jim said.

"No, I think I can get it," I said, pushing my fingers down as far as I could. Then I flinched and pulled my hand back. "Ow. Geez, that hurts." I shook my hand and noticed blood pouring out of a cut on my index finger. "Chef Claire, I'm gonna need a dish towel and some Band-Aids."

"You're gonna need some stitches," Chef Claire said, hopping out of her chair and heading for the kitchen.

"What the heck is in there?" Jim said, gently using a finger to explore the top of the opening.

"It's incredibly sharp whatever it is," I said, squeezing my finger and holding it over my head to stem the flow of blood.

Chef Claire returned carrying a damp dish towel. She wrapped it tight around my finger.

"You need to go to the emergency room?" Chef Claire said.

"No, just give Josie a call and tell her I need some stitches," I said.

I noticed the odd look both Jim and Mary were giving me.

"I didn't know vets could work on humans," Mary said.

"Well, they're not supposed to. But I'm fluent in dog, so…," I said, giving her a small smile.

They both snorted and shook their heads.

"Chef Claire, do you have a pair of scissors?" Jim said.

"Yeah, they're in the top drawer right over there," she said, nodding since she was using both hands to gently hold the dish towel in place. "Between you and Max, if Saturday doesn't hurry

94

up and get here, we're going to have to hold the reception in the ER."

"Funny," I said, lowering my hand and unwrapping the towel to take a look at my wound. Blood immediately began pouring out of the cut. I quickly rewrapped it. "Nope. Not quite ready for fresh air."

We watched Jim cut along the edge of the spine then heard a soft thump as a cloth bag fell onto the table.

"If it's what I think it might be, it's probably a good idea if you open the bag and pour out what's inside instead of using your hand," I said.

"You think it could be the murder weapon?" Jim said, untying the string at the top of the bag.

"I think it's a possibility. And it's certainly sharp enough," I said. "And if it is, there could be fingerprints on it."

He pulled the bag open and slid the object inside onto the table. The sound of metal hitting wood followed and we all stared, open-mouthed, at what resembled a letter opener about ten inches long. But it was the dazzling array of gemstones covering the handle that captured our attention.

"What the heck?" Jim said, leaning in close to inspect the item, but not touching it.

"I think we should call Chief Abrams," I said, reaching for my phone. I waited for the call to connect. "Chief, it's me…Yeah, I'm good. Hey, I think we might have located the murder weapon…No, I'm at Josie and Chef Claire's new place.

You should definitely swing by. And bring a fingerprint kit with you…No, we haven't touched it…Okay, we'll see you soon." I ended the call. "He's on his way."

"Should we go through the last binder?" Jim said.

"I don't see why not," I said, then looked at Chef Claire. "You got any gloves around?"

"I've got some rubber gloves in the kitchen. Hang on."

"We've probably already contaminated the prints on the other binders, but it might be worth trying to minimize the damage on this one."

Chef Claire returned carrying a pair of yellow rubber gloves. She handed them to Jim, and he pulled them on with a loud *snap*.

"It's a good look for you," Mary said to her husband. "Maybe you should try it out around the house."

"That's why we have a dishwasher, Mary," Jim said, making a face at her as he reached for the last binder.

We watched as he flipped through the individual pages. The inventory continued, and it was impossible to miss the fact that Charlie had paid healthy sums for several items. When he reached the end of the binder, a sealed 8 ½ by 11 envelope tucked inside the back pocket of the binder caught our eye. Jim grabbed the edge of the envelope, and it easily came loose. He placed it on the table in front of us. We all stared at it like little kids on Christmas morning.

"Aren't you going to open it?" Chef Claire said.

"I wonder if we should wait for the Chief," Jim said. "You know, in case it's something important."

"Good call," I said, leaning forward in my chair. "What do you think it is?"

"I have no idea," Mary said.

"Maybe it's an item he hadn't gotten around to adding to his inventory yet," Jim said.

"Could be," Mary said. "But Uncle Charlie didn't like to buy paper or handwritten items. He said it was too easy to get ripped off by people pushing counterfeit documents."

"Well, whatever it is, it's not very thick," Jim said.

We all glanced out the window when we heard Chief Abram's car pull into the driveway.

"He got here fast," Mary said.

"One of the benefits of living in a small town," I said, heading for the door to greet the Chief.

"How's the bride to be?" he said, following me back into the dining room.

"I'm great."

"What happened to your hand?"

"I stuck it someplace it didn't belong," I said. "Josie's on her way to stitch me up. You coming to the party tonight?"

"Well, I guess it depends on how the next few minutes go. Hi, guys," he said, glancing around to greet everyone. Then he focused on the collection of items strewn on the table. "What do you have for me?"

"The binders contain the inventory of all the memorabilia Charlie bought over the years," Jim said. "And the thing with all the gemstones on the handle is what cut Suzy's hand. We're not sure, but it could be the murder weapon."

"Did you bring your fingerprinting kit?" I said.

"I did," Chief Abrams said. "But unless there are prints on the blade, I doubt if I'll be able to lift any off the handle. Are those gemstones real?"

"We don't know," Mary said. "As soon as we found it, Suzy gave you a call."

"Okay," the Chief said. "Any idea what's in the envelope?"

"No," Jim said, shaking his head. "We thought you should be here as a witness before we opened it."

"Thanks. Good call," he said, reaching for his phone. "Chef Claire, if you wouldn't mind filming the opening of the envelope. I'd like to have a video record of it."

"Sure, Chief," Chef Claire said, accepting the phone from him.

"You're wearing the gloves, Jim, so why don't you do the honors?" Chief Abrams said. "You ready, Chef Claire?"

"Already recording, Chief."

The Chief nodded at Jim, and he picked the envelope up and slid his rubber-gloved index finger underneath the seal. Then he removed the document and set it down on the table in front of him.

"It's Uncle Charlie's will," Mary said, studying the first page. "The letterhead says William Johnson. He must have been the attorney Uncle Charlie used."

"Bill's been dead for a few years," Chief Abrams said. "And when he passed, his law practice died right along with him."

"Not gonna be much help," I said. "You know, as far as getting any more information about the will."

"No, it won't," the Chief said, shaking his head. "Jim, flip to the last page, please."

Jim complied and we all stared at the signature page.

"Two pages," he said. "Short and sweet."

"It's signed and notarized," the Chief said. "Looks like four years ago."

"That means it's legitimate, right?" Mary said to the Chief.

"Unless another will somehow turns up, I don't see why it wouldn't be," Chief Abrams said, then shrugged. "Okay, let's do some light reading."

Chapter 11

Josie arrived with her medical bag in hand before Jim could even get started reading. She knelt down to return Luna's warm and lengthy greeting then sat down next to me at the dining room table.

"What happened?" she said, unwrapping the dish towel. Then she grimaced when she saw the cut. "Geez. Nasty."

"I was trying to find out what was tucked inside the back of that binder," I said, studying my wound.

"I take it you found out the hard way," she said, filling a syringe with a numbing agent.

"Yeah, it was that thing," I said, nodding at the bejeweled object. "It looks like some sort of letter opener."

"You could use it as a letter opener," she said, injecting my finger in two places. "But that's not was it designed for."

"You know what it is?" Chief Abrams said.

"I do," she said. "I took an elective in college dealing with 19th and early 20th-century European artwork and artifacts."

"Really?" I said, frowning at her.

"Yeah, I registered late, and it was either art history or an orienteering class. I decided an air-conditioned classroom sounded a whole lot better than humping around the woods with a backpack and a compass."

"Good call," I said, flinching when she started her stitch work. "Hey, easy does it."

"Don't be such a baby," she said, focused on her work. "Anyway, what you're looking at is a miniature dagger often carried by government officials or wealthy business people. They were either worn around the belt or tucked inside the coat pocket. They were a status symbol, and, judging by the look of it, extremely effective at discouraging anyone trying to rob them."

"I can't believe people walked around carrying it," I said. "You'd end up stabbing yourself."

"The dagger was kept inside a scabbard," Josie said as she continued to efficiently sew my finger.

"Scabbard?" Jim said. "Like a pirate?"

"Yeah, pretty much," Josie said. "It was a sheath that protected the dagger. Usually made of metal with gemstones matching the handle." She paused to glance around the room. "Let me guess. You didn't find the scabbard?"

"No," Chef Claire said. Then she handed the phone to Mary. "If you don't mind taking over for a few minutes, Mary, I'll be right back."

Chef Claire headed for the cabinet, rummaged around for a few moments, then produced a flashlight. She headed upstairs two stairs at a time.

"There you go," Josie said as she tied off the final stitch and wrapped a bandage over the now-closed wound.

"How many?" I said, examining my finger.

"Only seven," she said, tossing everything back into her bag. "The good news is the bandage matches your wedding dress."

"Funny. Thanks for sewing me up," I said, focusing on the will. "You guys ready to hear what Charlie had to say?"

"Let's do it," Jim said, staring down at the document. Then he began reading. "I, Charles Merrihew, being of sound mind and body, and as witnessed by my lawyer, William Johnson, present this document as my last will and testament, signed and notarized on the date displayed on the signature page. This is the only version I have drafted of my will and, as such, it should be considered the sole and final basis for the disposal of my personal assets as outlined below."

"Uncle Charlie never talked like that," Mary said.

"It's pretty standard legalese," Chief Abrams said.

"Here we go," Jim said. "Item 1. To my brothers, Philip and Wilbur Merrihew, I leave absolutely nothing." Jim paused to glance at his wife. "Harsh."

"You saw them at dinner last night," Mary said. "Would you leave them anything?"

"Uh, no," Jim said, laughing, then continued reading from the will. "Given my brothers' constant whining, their walking around fully expecting to be given a handout simply because they somehow felt deserving, and the shabby treatment they gave my wife and me over the years, I believe they should receive from my estate exactly what they deserve. Which, again I repeat, is absolutely nothing. Nada, zip, bupkis."

"He's pretty clear," Mary said, laughing.

"He sure was. I doubt if anybody will try to contest it," Chief Abrams said.

"Oh, I'm sure they will," Jim said. "Item 2. To my beloved sister, Shirley Merrihew, I leave the antique set of porcelain figurines she has always admired. These items are outlined in the inventory of my collected artifacts as items 25-31."

Jim paused again and waited as Mary flipped through the first binder and located the items.

"There they are," Mary said. "No purchase price is listed. He must have got his hands on them during the war."

"I'm beginning to wonder how much time Charlie spent *fighting* over there," Jim said, shaking his head.

"He was wounded twice," Mary said.

"Probably got shot fleeing the scene of the crime," Jim said, half-serious.

"Stop it," Mary said, laughing. "Keep reading."

Chef Claire returned holding the flashlight in one hand and an object in her other. She placed it on the table next to the dagger, and we all stared at it in silence. The pattern of the gemstones perfectly matched the dagger's handle. It glittered from the light above the table.

"Where did you find it?" I said.

"It was under the armoire," Chef Claire said.

"Whoever killed Charlie used the dagger but managed to lose the scabbard?" the Chief said.

"The killer must have been up in the attic and heard us arrive," Chef Claire said. "Then they panicked, somehow managed to lose the scabbard, and took off."

"Take off from the attic?" the Chief said. "How the heck did they manage that?"

"Good question, Chief," Chef Claire said.

"By using the chain ladder," Mary said softly.

We all stared at her. Eventually, she continued.

"Uncle Charlie got it a long time ago," Mary said. "He was worried if a fire ever started while people were upstairs, they wouldn't have any way to get out of the house. He bought one of those metal chain ladders that hooks over the windowsill. I remember he used to make us practice climbing down. It always scared the crap out of me every time I had to do it."

"Did you see it while you were up there?" Chief Abrams said to Chef Claire.

"No, but I really wasn't looking," she said, shaking her head.

My neurons flared then eventually coalesced.

"He killed Charlie, but before he could get out of the house, he heard you guys downstairs and panicked. He found the chain ladder, but realized he wouldn't be able to climb down carrying the binders. And he also didn't relish the thought of trying to carry the dagger without the scabbard down the ladder."

"So, whoever it was, stuffed the dagger back into the cloth bag then hid it in the binder?" Jim said.

"That's what I'm thinking at the moment," I said. "And he planned to come back later, find the scabbard, grab the dagger and get out of the house." I looked at Mary. "Did everybody in the family know about the ladder?"

"They did," Mary said, nodding.

"It's weird," the Chief said. "But I can make it work."

"Yeah, me too," I said, then turned to Mary. "Where does the ladder take you?"

"Right down into the backyard," she said.

"It's pretty private back there, isn't it?" I said, trying to remember the yard from when I was a kid.

"Yeah, it is," she said. "Uncle Charlie loved his privacy."

"Almost as much as he hated his neighbors," Jim said.

"Look at it," I said, focusing on the scabbard. "Do you think those stones are real?"

"I'd be surprised if they weren't," Josie said. "Amazing array of stones. There's a bunch of diamonds, rubies, emeralds...I'm pretty sure the ones on both sides are sapphires."

"It's incredible," Jim said. "Is the big stone in the center a ruby? It looks different from the others."

"Holy crap," Josie whispered, staring at the gemstone Jim was referring to.

"What is it?" he said, glancing over at her stunned expression.

"Let me take a look," Josie said, sliding her chair closer to the table. "Are you kidding me?"

"What on earth is the matter with you?" I said, inching closer to her to get a closer look.

"What sort of stone does it remind you of?" Josie said to me.

"Well, from the shape, it looks exactly like a diamond. Except it's red," I said, shrugging.

"Exactly," Josie said, nodding.

"Is that supposed to mean something to us?" Chief Abrams said.

"I remember this stone from my art history course," Josie said.

"It's nice to see you were paying attention in class," I said. "But what the heck is it?"

"It's a red diamond," Josie said, then paused for effect.

"At the risk of repeating myself," the Chief said. "Is it supposed to mean something to us?"

"The red diamond is one of the rarest gemstones on the planet," Josie said.

"How rare?" Jim said.

"Rare enough to be worth up to a million bucks a carat," Josie said.

A lengthy silence ensued as everyone glanced at each other then down at the scabbard.

"Uncle Charlie had this thing and never said a word?" Mary said.

"I get it," Jim said. "If I owned something like this, I doubt if I'd be talking about it. Especially if I'd stolen it."

"And it's not only the gemstones," Josie said. "What you're looking at is undoubtedly a unique, one-of-a-kind artifact. Those two things combined make it incredibly valuable."

"Define incredibly valuable," Jim said, glancing over at Josie.

"Probably millions," she said, shrugging. "It's the best I can do."

"Close enough," Jim said. "And I have to say it raises one very important question."

"Who was he leaving it to?" I said.

Jim nodded then stared at Josie.

"What?" she said, returning his stare.

"I was waiting," he said, grinning.

"For what?"

"Isn't this the time when you usually say *nothing gets past you*?"

"I must be off my game today," Josie said, laughing. "Keep reading."

"Item 3," he said, again reading from the document. "To my son and daughter, Billy and Geraldine Merrihew, I leave my house and all other personal possessions not specifically addressed in this document. I hope in doing so, I can somehow begin to repay them for my considerable shortcomings as their father. I know I have caused both of them considerable pain over the years, made worse by my ongoing indifference and obstinance. Nothing can remove from their memories the stain of my fatherhood, and I would like to take this opportunity to apologize and tell them both, as hard it will be for them to believe me, I love them both very much."

"At least he made an effort," Mary said with a loud sigh.

"Yeah. But too little, too late," Jim said.

"Is that all of it?" Chief Abrams said after a long silence.

Jim turned back to the second page.

"No, there's one more," he said. "Item 4. To my beloved niece, Mary Cummings, who provided me endless love, support, and comfort for many years, I leave my most prized possession, identified as Item 47 in the inventory of my personal memorabilia."

"No way," Mary said, stunned and staring at the dagger and scabbard.

"There's only one way to find out," Jim said, reaching for the first binder and flipping through the pages. "Item 45, 46...48." He glanced up at his wife. "The plastic sleeve for item 47 is empty."

"You're joking," Mary said.

"Take a look for yourself," he said, sliding the binder across the table to her.

"Motive and the murder weapon in one shot," I said, staring at Chief Abrams. "Not a bad afternoon, huh?"

"Yeah, if you're right," he said. "But why would they take the page out of the binder?"

"Probably to do some research to see if they could find the history of what it is. And try to get some idea of what it's worth," Josie said.

"And if that's the only copy, maybe they figured they could keep the person Charlie was planning to give it to from taking possession of it," I said. "Does the will say anything else about it?"

"No," Jim said, shaking his head. "All it says is it was Item 47."

"Okay," Chief Abrams said. "I'm going to need some time to digest all of this. And I need to take all this stuff with me."

"You will keep a close eye on it, right, Chief?" Mary said, raising an eyebrow at him.

"I will," he said. "Your uncle wasn't going to be cremated, was he?"

"No, he wasn't."

"Okay," Chief Abrams said. "As soon as Freddie gets back from New York, he should be able to tie the wound to the dagger. And I'll get all this back to you as soon as possible."

"Thanks, Chief," Mary said, exhaling loudly. "This is a lot to deal with."

"We'll get through it," Jim said, patting her hand.

"We need to talk to Billy and Geraldine. As well as Uncle Phil and Uncle Wilbur. Aunt Shirley too."

A long silence ensued, and Chief Abrams and I shared a long stare. Jim noticed and put the question out there.

"You're reluctant to tell them about this, aren't you?" Jim said to Chief Abrams.

"In all honesty, yes, I am."

"Because you think one of them might have been the one who killed Charlie?" Jim said.

"Oh, that's nonsense," Mary said.

"Is it?" Jim said, glancing at his wife. "Is it possible Charlie shared his plans with any of them?"

"Anything's possible," she said. "Especially if Uncle Charlie had been drinking and they pissed him off. Yeah, I guess I can see him telling them. But killing him, Jim? C'mon, be serious."

"Stranger things have happened," he said. "Especially when it comes to families and money."

"But who? I mean, really, Jim."

"Well, you've got two brothers who shared a mutual hatred with Charlie," Jim said. "And a son whose father thought he shouldn't have ever been born."

"No way," Mary said, shaking her head.

"Not to mention the Graverobber," Jim said.

"Geraldine? Killing her own father? You're out of your mind."

"Maybe," Jim said. "But she one of the leading experts on historical artifacts, and if she found out her dad was leaving something to you that's worth millions, she might take it personally."

"Geraldine," I whispered.

"Yeah, the thought did cross my mind," Chief Abrams whispered back. "I hate to say this, but you two might want to be extra careful the next few days until we get a few things sorted out."

"What are you talking about?" Mary said. "We don't even know for sure Uncle Charlie was planning on giving it to me."

"Use your head, Mary," Jim said. "It's exactly what Charlie was planning to do. His most *prized possession*? I doubt very much if he was talking about a German army helmet."

"If the killer knows Charlie's plan was to give it to you, he or she might not think twice about trying to remove you from the equation," the Chief said.

"At the risk of sounding morbid, that raises an interesting question, Chief," Josie said.

"What?"

"If Mary and Jim were, God forbid, somehow taken out of the equation, who would inherit it?"

"I'm sure the lawyers could have a field day with it," Chief Abrams said. "But from what I heard Jim read, everything not specifically addressed in the will goes to Billy and Geraldine."

"And if we were gone," Jim said. "I imagine you could build a pretty good case it should go to Charlie's kids."

"You could," the Chief said, nodding in agreement. "All the more reason to be extra careful for a while."

"Great," Mary said. "I'm supposed to walk around worried about being stalked by members of my own family?"

"Try to think happy thoughts," Jim said.

"Like how much the thing is worth?" she said.

"Nothing gets past you," he said, staring at the dagger.

Chapter 12

I spotted Chief Abrams and his wife, Sue, strolling across my mother's backyard and headed straight for them. They came to a stop and gave me long, warm hugs. The guests were arriving in droves, and I wanted to have a quiet word with the Chief before I began mingling. I'd spent the last few hours forcing myself to relax and focus on my responsibilities as the bride-to-be, but my brain had been working overtime since we'd discovered the will and purported murder weapon.

"Suzy," Sue said, holding me by the shoulders and beaming at me. "You look fantastic. Are you getting excited for Saturday?"

"Thanks, Sue. I am. But I've got a lot on my mind I can't seem to shake."

The Chief gave me a sideways glance but said nothing.

"Completely understandable," she said. "Just take it one thing at a time. Before you know it, you and Max will be settled into your new life." She glanced around the lawn. "Where is he?"

"He's in New York with the boys," I said. "They'll be back tomorrow. How's Wally doing? I haven't seen him in ages."

Wally was their Basset Hound who stayed at the Inn when they were visiting their kids on the west coast or when Sue was traveling and the Chief got overloaded at work forcing him to leave the dog by himself for hours on end. It was something Wally hated.

"He's great," Sue said. "We dropped him off at the Inn before we headed over here."

"Really? You're not leaving town, are you?"

"No, not at all. Sammy offered to follow us back to the Inn after the party so we can pick him up," she said. "We're not sure what time we'll get home tonight, and we didn't want to leave him alone in the house. A couple of the neighbors are starting to lose their patience.

"Is his howling getting worse?" I said, surprised the Basset, now somewhere around four years old, hadn't grown out of the habit.

"Yeah," the Chief said, shaking his head. "He's such a big baby. If you walked by the house and heard him, you'd swear we were torturing him."

"We've been thinking about talking to you and Josie about ways we might be able to break him of the habit. It's a real problem. You got any ideas?"

"I do," I said, nodding. "Get another dog. I'm sure Wally is howling because he hates being alone. And I'm willing to bet if he has another dog around, he'll stop feeling so isolated."

"Another dog?" Chief Abrams said with a frown. "I don't know, Suzy. I'm worried we'd be doubling our problem. What happens if the other dog starts mimicking Wally?"

"Don't even go there," Sue said, laughing. "A lot of people say two dogs aren't any more work than one. Sometimes, even less."

"It can be," I said. "Tell you what, swing by the Inn next week and bring Wally with you. We'll put him out the play area with the rest of our gang and see who he bonds with. I'll let Josie know you're coming. She'll be able to tell you which dog would be a good fit."

"It's probably worth a shot," the Chief said, glancing at his wife.

"I like it," she said, waving to someone on the other side of the lawn. "There's your mom. I'm going to go say hi to her." She glanced back and forth at both of us. "Try to keep the shop talk to a minimum."

"Sure, sure," I said, giving her a quick hug before she headed off. "How do you it, Chief?"

"Do what?"

"Stay so happy after all these years," I said.

"I married the right woman," he said with a shrug. "And Max is doing the same thing."

"Aren't you sweet," I said, then rocked back and forth on my heels. "What did you find out?"

"I was going to ask you the same question," he said.

"Why would you ask me?" I said, toeing the grass with my sandal.

"Don't be coy," he said. "As soon as you left the house this afternoon, you went straight to your office to do some research on the dagger, didn't you?"

"Maybe."

"What did you find?" he said, gesturing for me to follow him across the lawn.

"I'm almost positive it's something called the Red Diamond Dagger," I said, veering toward a section of the lawn behind the area where the party was taking place. "Let's go sit in the maze so we can talk without being interrupted."

"Sounds like a plan," he said. "And after we chat, you're going to focus on the party, right? Your mother will kill me if she finds out we're talking about the case."

"Hence our decision to sit in the maze," I said, gently tugging his sleeve.

The maze was an area about the size of a football field my mother had created when I was a young girl. Similar to something we had seen in The Shining, a movie I'm still unable to watch by myself, it was comprised of large hedges offering a variety of ways to reach the inner circle; a sitting area complete with a fountain that doubled as a birdbath. It was easy to get lost and spend a half-hour wandering around in circles. While there are several paths you can use to reach the sitting area, there are only two exits to the maze itself. As a young girl, my friends and I made good use of the area to play hide and seek, cops and robbers, and a host of other childhood games. During the long winter months, we added snowball fights and snow forts into the mix. Every time I walked the maze, a host of childhood memories, as well as a few teenage memories of a more adult nature, always surfaced and put a smile on my face.

The best thing about the inner-circle was the privacy it offered. And privacy was what I was looking for at the moment. Since the Chief and I were about to discuss the possibility one of my childhood friends might have killed their father, the last thing I wanted was to be eavesdropped on.

"I'm glad you're leading the way," the Chief said, glancing up at the hedges that had grown to almost eight feet high over the years.

"We're almost there," I said, making a left followed by a quick right. We came to a clearing, and a fifteen-foot-square section appeared. Four wrought iron benches surrounded the gurgling fountain. I sat down and stared up at the night sky.

"I love this place," I said.

"It's unique," Chief Abrams said, draping a leg over his knee. "No doubt about it. Tell me about this Red Diamond Dagger."

"It's from back in the early 1900's," I said. "It was supposedly owned by Kaiser William. No, Wilhelm. At the end of the first World War, it went missing right around the time he did. People assumed he'd been buried with it, and, sometime during the 1930s, graverobbers decided to find out."

"They dug the guy up?" the Chief said, grimacing.

"Yeah, if you believe the rumors. Disgusting, huh? The dagger surfaced at some point and came into the possession of one of Hitler's henchmen. The details are a bit fuzzy about which one. But there was quite a battle for possession. Then it mysteriously disappeared again, and no traces of it have been seen or heard since then."

"How the heck did Charlie get his hands on it?"

"I've got no idea," I said. "Maybe it was a case of him being in the right place at the right time."

"And he kept quiet about it all these years?"

"It certainly looks like it," I said. "At least until recently."

"You think some of the family members learned about it?"

"They must have, right?" I said, tucking my legs underneath me on the bench. "I think Charlie made the decision to let one or more people know what we had. Knowing Charlie, he took great pleasure in telling his family he wasn't leaving it to any of them."

"Take pleasure in telling them what, darling?"

Both Chief Abrams and I jumped, startled by my mother's unannounced arrival.

"Geez, Mom. Don't do that."

"Do what?"

"Snoop on me," I said. "Now I know who I get it from."

"You've never needed my help, darling. What's going on?" she said, sitting down on the bench directly across from me. "You're supposed to be mingling."

118

"I am mingling," I said, playing defense. "I thought I'd start with the Chief."

"I see," she said, nodding. "Have you gotten to the time I caught you and Jeffrey Daniels out here during your junior year?"

"Now there's a story I'd love to hear," the Chief said, laughing.

"Shut it," I said, making a face at him. "We're mingling, Mom. Not reviewing our life histories."

"Start talking, young lady," she said, fixing her stare on me.

I did.

When the Chief and I finished bringing her up to speed, she merely nodded and continued to sit quietly.

"I see," she said, eventually.

"That's it?" I said, raising an eyebrow at her.

"What? Are you expecting me to break into a song and dance routine?"

"No. But you're way too calm. By now, you're usually telling me to mind my own business," I said.

"I'm sure you're right, darling," she said, sitting back on the bench. "But I made myself a promise nothing you did this week, short of calling off the wedding, was going to ruin my good mood."

"I'm impressed," I said, nodding.

"Don't get used to it," she said evenly. "And Charlie was a friend of mine for over forty years. The thought someone killed him makes my blood boil. How much do you think this Red Diamond Dagger might be worth?"

"Millions," Chief Abrams said.

"And Charlie's plan was to leave it to Mary?" my mother said.

"It was," I said, nodding. "But if the killer manages to get hold of the will and the dagger, Mary might not have any claim to it. Did Charlie ever mention anything to you?"

"No, Charlie was a very private man," she said. "But recently he'd made a few cryptic comments about how several of his family members weren't going to be happy with him."

"Do you think he told them what was in his will?" I said.

"I don't have a clue," she said with a shrug. "But I think his decision to leave it to Mary and Jim was a wonderful idea. They were very good to Charlie over the years."

"The will says everything not specifically called out in the document goes to Billy and Geraldine," the Chief said.

"That should tell you a lot," my mother said softly.

"You think one of them could have done it?" I said, shaking my head. "Being angry with your father is one thing. Killing him off is something else altogether."

"Billy? I seriously doubt it," she said. "He's never been motivated by money, and despite the way his father treated him, Billy always remained almost philosophical about their differences. No, I can't see Billy doing it. No matter how much the dagger is worth."

"Geraldine?" I said, tossing it out with enormous regret.

"I'm afraid Geraldine is a bit harder to take off my list of suspects," my mother said.

"You have a list too?" I said, surprised.

"I was speaking metaphorically, darling."

"You think she might have done it?"

"Well, given her line of work, if Charlie had told her about the dagger she would have known right away what it was."

"And what it might be worth," Chief Abrams said.

"Yes," my mother said. "She's always been different from Billy. And Geraldine would know how to unload it quietly. The circle of clients she deals with share two important qualities when it comes to acquisitions of this sort."

"They have a ton of money, and they value their privacy," I said, nodding.

"Well done, darling. And part of the privacy aspect includes knowing the importance of keeping your mouth shut," my mother said. "If this dagger is as special as you say it is, it's not the sort of thing you try to sell on eBay."

"But killing her own father over money?" I said, still refusing to believe it.

"Unlike you, darling, someone less motivated by money than anyone I've ever met, other people are different."

"I'm not motivated by it because I have more money than I know what to do with," I said with a shrug.

"It wouldn't matter, darling," she said. "You could be living on the street and still not care about it. As a motivator, anyway."

"Almost sounds like a compliment, Mom," I said, laughing.

"It's the best I can do when it comes to your relationship with money, darling."

A thought bubbled to the surface, and I looked at Chief Abrams.

"You talked to all the family members after Charlie was killed, didn't you?"

"I did," the Chief said. "And their alibis all checked out. But if two of them are working together, they could be covering for each other."

"They were all here in town, right?" I said.

"They were. All except for Geraldine who was in Toronto," he said.

"That's right," I said. "She changed her plans and landed there instead of Montreal. Jim was really cranky with her for not letting them know."

"I don't blame him," the Chief said. "I talked with Geraldine soon after she got to town. She'd spent the night in Toronto watching a show."

"Hamilton," I said, remembering the conversation. Another thought surfaced, and I grabbed my phone from my pocket. "I knew there was something I forgot to do." I searched for the touring schedule of the popular show and scrolled through the results. Then I exhaled loudly and shook my head.

"Geez," I whispered.

"What's the matter?" the Chief said.

"Take a look," I said, handing him my phone.

"Son of a gun," he said.

"What is it?" my mother said, leaning forward to read from the screen.

"Hamilton doesn't open in Toronto until next week," Chief Abrams said.

All three of us sat quietly for several moments.

"Why would she lie about that?" I said. "It's so easy to check."

"Who would ever even bother to check?" Chief Abrams said.

"If I were planning to kill somebody, I'd do everything I could to make sure I had an airtight alibi."

"People do dumb things," the Chief said. "Especially when they're under stress."

"I can't believe Geraldine was involved," I said in protest. "If anybody from the family did it, it had to be one or both of Charlie's brothers."

"Maybe they did do it," my mother said with a shrug. "For a cut of the profits. I wouldn't put it past either one of them. They're despicable."

"And dumber than a box of rocks," the Chief said. "They probably would have done it for beer money."

"While Geraldine walks away with millions," I said, rubbing my forehead. "I hate saying it, but I can make it work."

"Me too," the Chief said.

"Okay, darling," my mother said, getting to her feet. "I'll make a deal with you. Rather than let you send my blood pressure off the charts, I'm going to ignore every bit of snooping you and the Chief decide to do tonight. Consider it an early wedding present."

"I must be dreaming, Chief," I said, laughing.

"*But*," she said, raising a finger in warning. "Starting first thing tomorrow morning, until you are officially married, you have to agree to put all this aside and let Chief Abrams handle things on his own. Tomorrow night is the rehearsal dinner. Saturday is the wedding. For the next two days, I expect you to play the role of the blushing bride and be the model of decorum."

"Blushing bride? Geez, Mom. Bit of a stretch, wouldn't you say?"

"You know exactly what I'm talking about," my mother said. "And don't even think about trying to test me on this one, young lady. Do we understand each other?"

"Got it, Mom."

"Good. Now, let's go enjoy the party and do some actual mingling," she said, leading the way out of the maze. "Now, Chief, let me tell you about the time I caught Suzy out here with Jeffrey Daniels."

"Mom! Don't you dare."

"Consider it a warning shot across the bow, darling," she said, glancing over her shoulder at me. "You know, as a reminder of what might happen if you disobey me on this one. And don't forget, I'll be making a toast at the reception."

"Crap," I said, scuffing the dirt with my sandals as I fell back out of earshot.

Chapter 13

Still confused by my mother's willingness to have me spend the evening snooping, as well as cranky about her sharing my teenage exploits with Chief Abrams, I left the maze and spotted Josie and Chef Claire leaning against one of the temporary bars. They were sipping wine and surveying the large crowd.

"There you are," Josie said. "We thought you might have gotten cold feet and headed for the hills."

"Not a chance," I said, gently punching her on the shoulder. "I was chatting with the Chief and my mom."

"Then you definitely need a glass of wine," Chef Claire said.

"Uh, no," I said, glancing around the backyard. "I think I need to keep a clear head tonight."

"How's your mom holding up?" Josie said, finishing her wine and waving to the bartender for another.

"She's full of surprises tonight. She actually gave me her blessing to do some snooping around."

"About who might have killed Charlie?" Chef Claire said.

"Yeah. I got a one-night-only reprieve from the governor," I said, laughing.

"She's pretty shaken up about what happened to him," Josie said, handing Chef Claire a fresh glass.

"So what's your plan?" Chef Claire said, clinking glasses with Josie.

"I thought I'd make the rounds with the Merrihew family. Have you seen them?"

"Yeah, they're all here," Josie said. "But they're not hanging out together. Geraldine is over there talking with her Aunt Shirley. Charlie's brothers grabbed a bottle of bourbon and are sitting by themselves at the table over there."

"What about Billy and Séance?" I said, surveying the scene.

"They're around somewhere," Chef Claire said. "Neither one of them seems to be in a very good mood."

"I take it Séance recovered from her migraine," I said, eventually spotting the couple sitting by themselves having what appeared to be a heated conversation.

"Yeah," Josie said, shaking her head. "She said she spent the afternoon doing a lengthy meditation session using crystals."

"Crystals?" I said, frowning.

"Yeah," Chef Claire said, glancing at the couple. "I didn't know people still bought into that crap. It's so…"

"Seventies?" I said, laughing.

"Close enough," Chef Claire said. "But I think any enlightenment she found came straight from a pill bottle. She's whacked out on something.

"Okay, wish me luck," I said, then realized something was amiss. "Hey, where are the dogs?"

127

"I took them back to the Inn about a half-hour ago," Chef Claire said.

"Were they being a pain?"

"Not at all," Chef Claire said. "They were the hit of the party, but we couldn't keep people from feeding them."

"Yeah, all we need is a bunch of drunks giving them garlic chicken or letting them lick their chocolate mousse plates," Josie said.

"Good call," I said. "I'll see you guys in a bit."

I decided to start with Geraldine and her aunt. After stopping along the way to chat with various well-wishers, I finally made it to their table. Geraldine pulled a chair back and invited me to sit down.

"Your mother certainly knows how to throw a party," Geraldine said. "This is great."

"One of her many talents," I said. "How are you doing, Shirley?"

"I've been better," she said, obviously still grieving over the death of her brother. "But this is helping. Thanks for inviting us."

"I'm glad you could make it," I said, then frowned as I glanced at her brothers who were making short work of the bottle in front of them. "I hope my mother bought enough bourbon."

"Well, if there's one thing Phil and Wilbur have always agreed on it's free food and drink," Shirley said.

128

"Did you get the funeral arrangements finalized today?" I said to Geraldine.

"No, we're still working on them," she said, nodding. "The service is Monday. Billy and I wanted to have it on Sunday, but none of the churches could make it work. You know, given their schedule of Sunday services."

"Yeah," I said, nodding.

"If you two will excuse me," Shirley said, getting to her feet. "I see a few old friends I haven't seen in ages. I'll let you two catch up."

"She's amazing," Geraldine said, watching her aunt stroll across the lawn. "How she managed to stay normal growing up around her siblings is still a mystery."

"Don't be modest, Geraldine," I said, smiling at her. "You seem to have managed it quite well yourself."

"I suppose."

"We haven't really had a chance to catch up since you got here," I said.

"No, we haven't," she said, smiling at me. "Getting married on Saturday. Good for you. You've come a long way, Suzy Chandler."

"What about you? Do you have anyone special in your life?"

"I do," she said, nodding.

"Do I hear wedding bells in your future?"

"I seriously doubt it," she said. "I don't think his wife would approve."

I flinched but quickly recovered.

"You're involved with a married man?"

"I sense judgment," she said, forcing a small laugh.

"Oh, you caught that?"

"It was a little hard to miss. But if it's any consolation, I didn't know he was married at first."

"He lied to you?" I said, frowning.

"No. It didn't come up at the time," Geraldine said, shrugging it off. "You know, we didn't talk much at first."

"Got it," I said. "You're serious about this guy?"

"Very much so," she said, tearing up.

I waited patiently until she composed herself then continued.

"Is he planning on getting divorced?" I said as gently as I could manage.

"It's very complicated. And it would be incredibly expensive for him."

"I take he's well off," I said.

"Oh, yeah," she said, shaking her head. "But the money is only part of the problem."

"What does he do?"

"Well, let's say he's a well-known celebrity and leave it there," Geraldine said. "As such, our situation is in limbo for the immediate future. At the moment, we've been reduced to the occasional encounter when we can make our travel schedules work."

"This might sound insensitive, but do you ever wonder if he might be playing you?"

"Only about a dozen times a day," she said, laughing.

"It has to be hard to deal with," I said.

"It ain't easy," she said, taking a sip of wine. "But our occasional encounters are still making up for it. So far."

"Okay," I said, sensing the need to switch topics. "Are you heading back to L.A. from here?"

"Eventually," she said. "But first I'm heading to Boston then Baltimore."

"Do you have clients there?" I said.

"Something like that," she said, deflecting the question and glancing away momentarily.

My neurons flared, and I immediately chastised myself for turning suspicious. I decided to push the conversation a bit despite my reservations.

"Can I ask you a question, Geraldine?"

"Suzy, I've known you since we were little kids," she said, laughing. "And I can't remember a single time you ever asked for permission."

"Yeah, well, it's something I've been working on," I said with a small shrug.

"Go right ahead," she said, leaning back in her chair.

"Who do you think might have killed your dad?"

"Wow, getting right to it, huh?"

"Yeah, I'm on kind of a tight schedule," I whispered.

"What?"

"Nothing," I said. "I ask because it's been driving me crazy. I can't believe anybody could kill your dad. Especially…" I trailed off, red-faced with embarrassment.

"Especially since it could have been someone from my family?" Geraldine said, raising an eyebrow.

"Yeah," I whispered. "Sorry. I'm being rude."

"No, only your usual inquisitive self," she said, gently swirling the wine in her glass. "But to answer your question, I have a few people in mind."

"You do?" I said, leaning forward in my chair.

"Yes," she said. "But what I don't have a clue about is *why* anybody would want to do it."

"I've found it's usually love or money," I said.

"Lack of love, maybe," she said with a small, sad chuckle. "And unless Dad had been holding out on us, I'm not sure there was enough money to get anybody's attention. Except for maybe the Bourbon Brothers over there."

I beat back the rush of adrenaline and forced myself to stay calm.

"Your uncles?"

"Can you think of any better suspects?" she said, studying my face closely.

"I guess it would depend."

132

"Oh, situational suspects. The plot thickens. Depend on what?"

"I guess on who knew what the whole story was," I said.

"The whole story?" she said, nodding. "Now, there's an interesting theory. What do you think the whole story might be?"

"I don't know," I said, shrugging the question off. "But most people usually have some secrets they keep to themselves. Maybe your dad had a few he had recently shared with the wrong people."

"Please don't take this the wrong way, Suzy, but what the hell are you talking about?"

"I'm wondering if your dad had recently started putting his affairs in order and mentioned them to you or Billy. Or maybe he said something to his siblings that rubbed them the wrong way."

"Why do I get the feeling there's something you're not telling me?" she said, now suspicious and edgy.

"This is a very delicate conversation, Geraldine," I said. "I'm trying to make some sense of what happened to your dad without coming across as insensitive."

"Maybe you should try again," she snapped. "You're fishing. You can't possibly believe Billy or I had anything to do with it."

"I'm sorry, Geraldine. This is a hard thing to talk about with anyone, especially someone who's been a good friend for a very long time."

My comment seemed to calm her down for the moment, and she tossed back the last of her wine.

"Yes, we have been friends a long time, haven't we? You think my dad had some money stashed away?" she said, sliding the empty glass away.

"I think it's possible he could have had some things other members of the family wanted to get their hands on," I said.

"Like what?"

"Something in his inventory of memorabilia."

"You saw all his crap this morning," she said, scowling. "Did you see anything valuable enough to justify killing somebody over?"

"No, I didn't."

Technically, it wasn't a lie since we hadn't come across the dagger until sometime in the afternoon. But it didn't minimize the guilt I was feeling. I looked at her and exhaled loudly.

"Well, thank you for a very weird conversation, Suzy," she said, getting to her feet. "I'm going to grab another glass of wine."

"I'm sorry, Geraldine. I didn't mean to upset you. I'm only trying to make sense of things."

"So am I. But I'm not the one walking around making insinuations to my friends in the process."

"Got it," I whispered.

"I'm going to chalk this conversation up to a case of pre-wedding jitters. You know, emotional overload coupled with a bunch of unanswered questions. Despite how our little chat is ending, I enjoyed catching up. Just like the good old days, huh? Talking about our boyfriends, or lack thereof. Wondering what life has in store for both of us." She stared off into the distance. "Maybe they're right. Maybe you shouldn't try to put the cork back in the bottle after it's been opened."

"Again, I'm so sorry I upset you, Geraldine."

"It's okay, Suzy. Friends forgive each other when they do stupid stuff," she said, still annoyed. "And sometimes they're forced to forgive each other before they know the whole story."

"What?"

"It's a general observation," she said, glancing around for the nearest bar. "Obviously there's something going on you're not willing to share. Or you're having problems dealing with the fact I'm involved with a married man."

"No, that's not it, Geraldine. People come into your life when you least expect it, right? Max and I literally ran into each other at a restaurant in Mexico."

"But at a time when neither one of you was involved with anyone else."

"No, we weren't."

"Therein lies the difference, *my friend*," she said.

I flinched when I caught the caustic tone in her voice.

"Maybe things will work out."

"It would require a small miracle," she said.

"Stranger things have happened," I said with a grin.

"You mean like my father getting stabbed in the neck?" she snapped. "Happy hunting, Suzy."

My smile disappeared in a flash. Not waiting for a response, she wheeled around and headed straight for the bar. I watched her walk away and exhaled loudly.

"That could have gone better."

Chapter 14

With the most difficult conversation out of the way, an encounter that had started well, gone south in a hurry, then managed to stabilize before I did irreparable damage to our friendship, I decided to see if Geraldine's brother might be able to offer some insight. I wasn't sure if the source of Geraldine's anger came from my reaction to the news of her affair with the unnamed celebrity or whether she had taken my circular questions as an accusation of her possible involvement in her father's murder.

If I was honest with myself, it was probably a bit of both.

I was still having a hard time believing she was capable of taking another person's life, especially the man who had raised her, did his best in his own strange way to teach her right from wrong, and provide for her and her brother. But I was also having a hard time putting aside the fact the Red Diamond Dagger was directly related to her career as a procurer of rare artifacts. And with several million dollars at stake for an item she might logically assume should be hers, sadly, I could make it work.

The nagging thought, while it might offer testimony to my powers of deduction, probably made me a crappy friend. Another wave of guilt-ridden, self-loathing washed over me as I

glanced around the crowded lawn. I finally spotted Billy and
Séance sitting by themselves near one of the bars. Judging by the
number of empty glasses on the table, they'd been taking
advantage of its proximity.

I worked my way through the crowd and stopped several
times to chat with various guests. I hadn't seen some of them in
years, and my progress was slow. Halfway across the lawn,
Chief Abrams and his wife waved me over.

"There she is," Chief Abrams said, giving me an evil grin.
"The Teenage Terror of Clay Bay."

I flinched at the nickname my mother had bestowed on me
when I was sixteen soon after she had popped into the sitting
area of the maze where Jeffrey Daniels and I were getting better
acquainted.

"Don't start," I said, glaring at him.

"I told her it was such a good story, she should weave it into
her toast at the reception," the Chief said.

"Leave her alone," Sue said. "You never did anything
embarrassing when you were a teenager?"

"Sure," the Chief said. "But not in front of my mother."

"Don't listen to him, Suzy," she said, scowling at her
husband. "I'm going to get another drink. Can I get you
anything?"

"Maybe a muzzle for him," I said, nodding at the Chief.
"No, I'm good."

"I'll be right back," she said as she headed off.

"Sorry," Chief Abrams said, still grinning. "I couldn't resist. How did your conversation with Geraldine go?"

"Not well. Between my questions about what might have happened to her dad, combined with my reaction to the affair she's having with a married man, it kind of went downhill in a hurry."

"She came right out and told you about the affair?"

"When we were in high school, we used to tell each other everything," I said. "Old habits die hard, I guess."

"Who's she having the affair with?" the Chief said.

"She wouldn't say. But he's a well-known celebrity. My guess is he's worried about having to give half of his money away, or he's stringing her along."

"Well, she does live in L.A," the Chief said with a shrug. "And in her line of work, she probably deals with folks like that all the time." He fixed his stare on me. "So, what's your take?"

"Do I think she killed her father?"

"Yeah."

"I don't know," I said, shaking my head. "But I sure hope not."

"I thought I might swing by and have a little chat with her," Chief Abrams said, glancing around the party. "How was she when you finished talking?"

"Cranky and suspicious. When I started asking questions about who could have done it, she gave me *the look*. It made the hairs on the back of my neck stand up."

"Thanks for winding her up. I'll check in with you later."

He gave me a small wave as he began working his way through the crowd. I continued my slow trek toward Billy's table. When I finally reached him and Séance, Billy glanced up with a smile and immediately pulled a chair out for me.

"There's the guest of honor," he said. "Terrific party."

"Thanks. But my mom handled everything," I said, then looked at Séance. "How's your migraine?"

"It's manageable at the moment," she said, scowling at her boyfriend.

"Have I come at a bad time?" I said, about to leave.

"No, not at all," Billy said. "Séance and I were talking about work."

"Or the lack thereof," she said, getting to her feet. "I need a drink."

She wandered off without fanfare, and I watched as she shouldered her way through the crowd.

"Are you sure she's okay?" I said.

"She'll be fine."

It sounded like he was trying to convince himself more than me, but I let it go without comment.

"She seems...fragile."

"Séance is an artist with an artist's sensibilities."

"Sure, sure," I said, again floundering with the conversation. "Can I ask you a question?"

"Of course."

140

"Why all the resistance about moving to L.A.?"

"You sound like Geraldine," Billy said, laughing.

"It does seem to make some sense," I said. "I'm no expert, but there's so much good television being made these days, one would think you'd both have a lot more options out there."

"Yes, one would think."

"And the weather is certainly a lot better."

"Séance hates the sun," Billy said. "She says it accelerates the aging process."

"Yeah, I get that. You gotta keep the instrument in tune for as long as you can, right?"

"Indeed. And it's especially true for women," he said. "It's not fair, but it's definitely a reality. Besides, Séance hates the thought of doing television. Considers it beneath her talents as an actress."

"I didn't think actors could be picky until after they'd made it."

"Touché," he said, nodding in agreement. "We've had the conversation many times."

"Without any success, right?"

"Not a bit," he said, giving me a small smile. "So, for the foreseeable future, it's New York for us. What's the matter?"

"I'm having a hard time with the idea she would take L.A. off the table. You know, not do everything she can to get acting work."

"Séance is convinced she has the right career strategy," Billy said. "Her plan is to keep doing stage work, pick up some showcase roles, and then get *discovered*."

"Discovered by someone who can put her in movies?"

"Yeah," he said, nodding.

"Well, at least she has a plan."

He took a sip of his beer then looked at me.

"Can I tell you a little secret?"

"A real secret I can't tell anybody or something I can only tell a couple of people?" I said, laughing.

"As long as it doesn't get back to Séance, I don't care who you tell," he said, laughing along.

"Ooh, my kind of secret. What is it?"

"The real reason Séance refuses to move to L.A."

"I'd love to hear it."

"She's scared. L.A. frightens her to death," he said, picking at the label on his beer bottle.

"Really? Why on earth would she be scared?"

"She thinks she's too old to try and get started all over in Los Angeles," he said.

"Too old? You said she was only thirty-four," I said, genuinely surprised.

"She's actually thirty-eight. But don't you dare breath a word about it to anyone."

"Oh, a *real* secret," I said.

"Exactly. Séance is convinced she can't compete with the constant influx of fresh faces who move to L.A.," Billy said. "And she might be right."

"So until she's discovered, it's off-Broadway plays mixed in with musicals?"

"Musicals?" he said, finding my comment funny. "Séance can't sing a note, and she's a terrible dancer. She's pretty much stuck with traditional stage work."

"Is there's much of it available?"

"There's some," he said, nodding. "But a lot of it gets snapped up by more established actresses looking to take a break from films."

"It sounds like she's caught between a rock and a hard place," I said.

"Yeah," he said, exhaling. "And every year she gets squeezed a little harder. It's become a major problem for her." He paused to take a long sip of beer. "And us."

"I'm sorry, Billy," I said. "Where did you two meet?"

"At an acting workshop," he said. "She was straight off the bus from Arkansas. Do you believe in love at first sight?"

I flashed back to the moment when Max and I had literally bumped into each other at a restaurant and smiled at the memory.

"I do."

"That's how it was for me," he said. "But it took her a long time to take me seriously. Eventually, I managed to convince her I was the right guy."

"By promising to support her?" I said, knowing the question was potentially crossing the line.

He gave me an odd look, then shrugged.

"When you boil it down, yeah. It's probably what it was all about. At least, from her perspective. She always said she would do anything necessary to avoid having to go back to her father's pig farm."

"Pig farm?"

"Yeah, her old man has a pig farm outside of Little Rock," Billy said. "Séance doesn't like to talk about it since she's done everything she can to reinvent her past. It's something I fully understand. You know, given my own somewhat disastrous childhood. She swears up and down she'll never set foot in a slaughterhouse again."

"She worked on the farm?"

"Of course," he said. "Everybody in her family worked. From a young age."

"Hence, her visceral reaction to bacon?"

"Exactly. She calls it a health choice, but the fact is it simply brings back a ton of bad memories."

"Can I ask you another question?"

"You haven't changed a bit, have you?" he said with a smile.

"Yeah, sorry."

"What do you want to know, Suzy?"

"She seems to have a permanent glazed look on her face. What's she using?"

He flinched and frowned at me.

"Is it obvious?"

"Pretty much."

"Prescription meds and booze," he said with a shrug. "It's a problem."

"It's obvious the situation is wearing on you. Why do you put up with it?"

"Fair question," he said. "Because I love her. And I understand her dream."

"But what about your dreams?"

"You have been talking to Geraldine, haven't you?"

"Not about that," I said.

"I still have some time," he said. "My window will be open for a while longer."

"Noble."

"Maybe," he said. "Or stupid on my part. But the good news is I'm going to inherit a bit of money from dear old Dad. I'm sure it won't be a lot, but it should take some of the pressure off for a while."

"Or you could use it as seed money to set yourself up on the west coast."

"I could," he said, nodding. "But I probably won't. It's amazing what having a bit of money does for one's peace of mind. But look who I'm talking to. You certainly don't need me to explain the concept to you."

"No, I don't. I'm blessed. And my mom is a genius with money."

"You'll never have to worry about it, will you?" he said, leaning forward in his chair.

"No. And neither will my kids. Or their kids, either," I said as a simple statement of fact.

"What's it like? Sometimes I fantasize about what a sudden windfall could do for my situation," he said.

I studied his face closely.

"I've never dealt with a windfall," I said. "At least one that made any difference to how I live. Having money removes a major worry most people spend their lives dealing with. But there's always a ton of other things to worry about."

"There are," he said, nodding. "But money can fix a lot of those, right?"

"I'd rather not talk about my money, Billy," I said. "As hard as it might be for you to believe, it's something I struggle with. For different reasons."

He stared at me then slowly nodded his head.

"Yeah, I imagine you do," he said. "You always had a sensitive soul. And you spent a lot of time looking out for kids like me. I always appreciated it."

"You're easy to like, Billy," I said, patting his hand. "And it was clear early on you and your dad were having a tough time dealing with each other."

"Dad never understood," he said, his voice breaking. "He thought I was nuts to pursue an acting career. He was convinced I was going to end up broke living on the street." He laughed, but it sounded more ironic than funny. "And who knows, by the time it's all said and done, he might have been right."

"Don't go there, Billy," I said, then decided it was time to change the subject. "When was the last time you talked to your dad?"

"It was only a couple of weeks ago," he said. "One day, he called me out of the blue. He had to call Geraldine first to get my number."

"What did you talk about?" I said, giving him my undivided attention.

"It was a weird conversation," he said, shaking his head. "He asked me if I was coming to your wedding. He said he'd been putting his affairs in order and had decided to leave the house to Geraldine and me. Then he laughed and said, if I found myself homeless, I was welcome to live here even though there wasn't much call for *so-called actors* up here in the North Country. Couldn't even deliver what he considered to be good news without taking another shot at me. Séance was furious when she heard him say it. I think it reminded her of how her father always talks to her."

"Séance was listening in on the conversation?"

"I'd been waiting to hear about a couple of callbacks. When I answered the phone, I put it on speaker without even checking the number."

"I take it the call didn't go well," I said.

"It was his usual barrage of cheap shots and jokes, then he mentioned the house. And he said something really strange about how he wished he could do more, but he felt compelled to do something nice for the people who truly cared about him."

"What was he talking about?"

"I'm not sure," he said. "My guess is he decided to leave a bunch of his crap to Aunt Shirley. She was always his favorite. But unless his will turns up, I guess we'll never know what his real intentions were. I told Aunt Shirley she's more than welcome to anything she wants."

"Yeah, the will," I said, my stomach again sinking for having agreed not to disclose what I knew. "Is that all he said?"

"Pretty much," Billy said, shrugging. "But toward the end of the conversation, he made some bizarre comment about the value of having dangerous jewelry. It didn't make any sense. I figured he'd started drinking early."

"The value of dangerous jewelry?" I whispered.

"Yeah, a weird thing to say, huh?"

"Can't argue with you," I said.

"That was my dad. Weird right to the end. So, where are you guys honeymooning?" he said, searching for a less painful topic.

"We're taking a boat down the River to Montreal. After a few days there, we're flying to Paris for ten days."

"Nice," he said, nodding. "Max seems like a good guy."

"He's great," I said, smiling as I wondered how his evening in New York was going. "I'm a lucky woman. Everybody deserves someone sweet and kind, right?".

"Indeed," he said, staring off into the distance. "I couldn't agree more."

His expression turned dark for a second before he fixed a smile on me.

"Somebody has to get lucky. It's the way things work," he said. "Congratulations, again. It couldn't happen to a nicer person."

"Thanks, Billy. Hang in there. I'm sure it's gonna turn around for you soon. You're too talented for it not to."

"See?" he said, downing the last of his beer. "Exactly what I was talking about. Nice." He pushed his seat back and stood up. "I need to go find Séance. It was great catching up with you, Suzy."

"You too, Billy."

I watched him weave his way through the throng of partygoers until he reached his girlfriend who was standing by herself at the bar. He placed a hand on her shoulder she shook off with a scowl.

I wasn't the only one who deserved a little sweet and kind.

Chapter 15

Feeling a bit better about myself thanks to Billy's kind words, I shook off a wave of melancholy and glanced around the party. I spotted Charlie's brothers sitting at a table by themselves. They appeared to be surly, both with each other as well as anyone who happened to stop by their table for a chat. The bottle of bourbon in front of them on the table was almost empty, and I realized I had to get over there soon if I wanted to have a coherent conversation with them. But since the Chief had mentioned he would be speaking to them, I decided it would be a good idea to get an update from him before I made my way to the sullen pair.

I began working my way through the partygoers, many of them on semi-tilt by this point in the evening and spent fifteen minutes accepting genuine well-wishes and coy comments about my upcoming wedding night and honeymoon. I took everything in stride, offered my thanks, then continued shouldering my way toward the bar where the Chief was chatting and laughing with Josie and Chef Claire.

"Wow," I said after I made my way across the lawn. "I've had easier treks through the woods. Brutal."

"It looked like quite a workout," Josie said, reaching for her wine glass.

"Yeah," I said, nodding. "I'm gonna count it." I focused on Chief Abrams who was keeping a close eye on the bourbon-swilling brothers. "How's it going?"

"I had an interesting chat with those two," he said, turning his attention to me.

"And?"

"Well, let's say I wouldn't put anything past them," he said, reaching for his glass.

"Did they mention if they'd spoken with Charlie recently?" I said, sneaking a glance at their table.

"They did," the Chief said. "Last week, in fact. And they weren't shy about telling me it hadn't gone well."

"Because?" I said, raising an eyebrow.

"I think something Charlie said to them derailed the conversation."

"I'm gonna guess it was something personal."

"Yeah, apparently they had been talking about old age and how hard it was to be looking straight down the barrel at a very short candle. It sounded like a lot of the usual stuff you hear at funerals and class reunions. How fast it all goes. I can't believe it's been fifty years, blah, blah, blah. Regrets about things none of them ever got around to doing. I think Phil and Wilbur took it as an opportunity to steer the conversation toward the need to put one's affairs in order while there was still time."

"But Charlie didn't bite?" I said, grabbing a handful of peanuts from a bowl on the bar.

"Haven't I taught you anything?" Chef Claire said, shaking her head.

"What are you talking about?" I said, glancing over at her.

"Eating from bowls of snacks sitting out on the open. It's germ central. You might as well let a hundred people breath all over you," Chef Claire said. "It's disgusting."

"We have bowls of stuff sitting on the bar at C's all the time," I said.

"Yeah, but have you ever seen me eating any of it?" she said, still frowning.

"As a matter of fact," I said, giving it some thought. "I don't think I have. But I have bigger things to worry about tonight."

"Okay," Chef Claire said. "But if you get sick on your honeymoon, don't blame me."

"Thanks for the warning," I said, gently punching her on the shoulder. I refocused on Chief Abrams. "What did Charlie say when his brothers steered the conversation to putting his affairs in order?"

"He told his brothers the only thing he could ever see himself leaving them was in the dust when they were hitchhiking on the side of the road," Chief Abrams said, laughing.

"Ouch," I said, laughing along.

"That's so Charlie," Josie said, reaching for a handful of peanuts. She caught the look Chef Claire was giving her then shrugged. "Hey, it's why they give us an immune system. I like to make sure it gets a regular workout."

"Oh, I'm sure it'll be working out. But I doubt if you're going to like it," Chef Claire said, then turned to the Chief. "Do you think the brothers know about the dagger?"

"I couldn't tell," he said. "But Phil did say at one point he was certain there had to be at least *one thing* of value in Charlie's collection of junk. His words, not mine."

"How did Wilbur react when he said it?" I said.

"He gave his brother a knowing smile and a nod. I think he wanted to say something but couldn't get his mouth working."

"They're still on your list of suspects?" Josie said.

"They certainly didn't say or do anything to make me take them off it," Chief Abrams said. "But I'm starting to lean in another direction."

"Geraldine?" I said, making solid eye contact with him.

"She's the one," he said, taking a sip of what appeared to be scotch on the rocks. "She immediately turned defensive as soon as I mentioned her dad."

"I wound her up pretty good," I said. "That might explain it."

"It could," he said, shrugging. "But when you put the existence of the dagger next to what she does for a living and add her relationship with her father to the mix, it's a pretty compelling argument. Especially if she learned her old man was planning on leaving it to Mary."

"Millions of dollars going to a cousin instead of the daughter?" Josie said. "Yeah, I can make it work."

"No, I still can't believe Geraldine could have done it," I said.

"Well, you know her a lot better than I do," Josie said, sliding her glass toward the bartender for a refill. "You sure you don't want a drink?"

"No, thanks. I've still got some snooping to do," I said, glancing around the lawn. "What about Charlie's sister, Shirley?"

"What about her?" Chief Abrams said.

"Do you think it's possible she might have been involved?"

Chief Abrams almost choked on a mouthful of scotch.

"Shirley? Have you completely lost your mind?"

"It wouldn't be the first time," I said.

"Suzy, she was a kindergarten teacher for forty years," the Chief said. "Not to mention the fact she also teaches Sunday school."

"A Sunday school teacher? How do you know that?" I said.

"She told me when we were chatting earlier," he said. "No way she was involved."

"Then who else could it be?" I said, my voice rising a notch.

"I have no idea," the Chief said, then lowered his voice. "And it's why I like Geraldine for it."

"No. It has to be somebody else," I said. "She couldn't do that." I glanced around at all three of them but waited in vain for a response. "Could she?"

"I don't know what to tell you, Suzy," the Chief said. "And there's a good chance we're never going to know. Unless Charlie's killer decides he can't let it go."

"With the will and the dagger, there's lots of motive. And plenty of opportunity," I said.

"Yeah, plenty of both," he said. "But no proof."

"Have you talked to Jim and Mary tonight?" I said, spotting them standing nearby chatting with my mother and Paulie and a few of their friends.

"Don't even go there, Suzy," Chef Claire said.

"I'm not going anywhere," I snapped, then immediately felt bad about doing it. "I'm sorry, Chef Claire."

"Don't worry about it," she said. "But before you go over a cliff jumping to conclusions, there is absolutely no way Jim and Mary were involved. They took care of the guy for close to twenty years."

"I'm not suggesting anything," I said, now playing defense. "I merely asked if you had talked with them tonight."

"Okay, guys," Josie said. "This is supposed to be a celebration. How about we dial it down a bit?"

"Good idea," the Chief said, scowling at me. "I agree with Chef Claire. If you're going to keep looking for Charlie's killer, when it comes to Jim and Mary, I suggest you look elsewhere."

"I wasn't accusing them," I said, glancing back and forth at them. "Why don't you people listen to what I'm saying?"

This time I was loud enough to draw the attention of several people standing nearby and I blushed before glancing around the immediate vicinity and forcing a smile.

"What on earth is the matter with you?" Josie said, making solid eye contact.

"I simply refuse to believe Geraldine had anything to do with her father's death," I whispered.

"Then there's a simple answer to your problem," she said. "Do everything you can to help the Chief figure out who did."

"What do you think I'm trying to do?" I said, my voice rising again despite my best efforts to control it.

"Drive all of us nuts?" Josie deadpanned.

Chief Abrams and Chef Claire both laughed. I initially fumed at the comment, then nodded at my maid of honor and gave her a hug.

"Sorry," I said to them.

Mary and Jim approached, and they both raised their glass in salute to me.

"To the bride," Jim said.

"Thanks."

"Great party," Mary said. "Your mom puts on quite a spread."

"Yeah, she's outdone herself," I said, making a mental note to swing by and thank her again.

"What are you guys talking about?" Jim said, glancing around. "We couldn't help but hear some loud voices."

"The usual stuff," Chief Abrams said.

"Like who might have killed Charlie?" Jim said.

"Yeah, pretty much," the Chief said.

"Well, as someone who reads a ton of mysteries, one thing I've learned it's usually the last person you'd suspect," he said with a conspiratorial wink.

It set my neurons on fire, and I immediately chastised myself and scuffed the grass with the toe of my sandal.

"If you have any ideas, be sure and let us know," Chief Abrams said, half-serious.

"Oh, I have a few ideas," Jim said.

"Please don't start," Mary said to her husband. "This is supposed to be a party."

"I'm multi-tasking," Jim said with a grin then took a sip of wine. "But I don't think you're going to be able to get a confession out of them tonight." He nodded in the direction of the bourbon-brothers who were passed out at their table. "Ah, the drunken slumber of the guilty."

"Jim, please stop," Mary said as she flashed her husband a disapproving glare.

"Sorry," he said. "I'm merely following the thread."

"Well, keep your threads to yourself," she said, then looked at the Chief. "He's convinced those two were behind it."

"It seems to be as good a theory as any other."

"Thank you, Chief," Jim said.

I spotted Billy and Séance making their way across the lawn.

"I'll be right back," I said. "I need to say goodbye to Billy and his girlfriend."

I quickly worked my way through the crowd and caught up with them before they reached the path leading down to the street. It was obvious whatever argument they'd been having earlier was still in progress.

"You guys taking off?" I said.

"I am," Séance said, staring off into the distance with an angry look on her face.

"Let me drive you back to the hotel," Billy said, placing a hand on her elbow she quickly shook off.

"No, it's quite all right. I walk all the time. I live in *New York,* and it's what New Yorkers do. And it's not going to change," Séance said, finally making eye contact with me. "Thank you for the party. I've had a lovely evening."

She wheeled around and headed down the path.

"If this is what she considers a lovely evening, I don't want to be around when she's having a bad night," I said softly.

"Yeah, tell me about it," Billy said, shaking his head as he stared after her. "A half-hour ago she finally started to relax. Then she got a text from her agent."

"Not good news I assume."

"No, Séance had gotten her hopes up about an audition she'd done last week. She was expecting a callback."

"But she didn't get it?"

"No, they decided to cast somebody else. An actress from L.A. with a serious resume in film and TV."

"Would I know her?"

"Oh, yeah," Billy said, thoroughly depressed. "But her name doesn't matter. It's the fact she's established and from L.A. is what set Séance off."

"Got it," I said, nodding. "What are you going to do, Billy?"

"I'm going to deal with whatever comes up," he said. "The same thing I always do."

"Can I ask you a question?"

He softly chuckled and shook his head at me.

"Sure. Why stop now?"

"Would you move to Los Angeles if Séance was out of the picture?"

"In a heartbeat. But I'm stuck for the moment."

"Yeah, I get it," I said. "You're in love, and you made a commitment."

"Yup," he said. "Pity the commitment is a bit one-sided at the moment."

"Well, hang in there," I said, doing my best to be supportive even though I believed his best option was to hop on the first plane heading west. "It has to get better."

"All I need to do is get my hands on some serious money," he said flatly. "You wouldn't think it would be that hard to do, right?"

Chapter 16

We had closed C's for the evening, and the dining room was packed for the rehearsal dinner with close to a hundred people. When we put together the guest list, I had mildly protested to my mother it was a large number of people to invite. She had listened then shrugged it off. Now, looking around the crowded room, I would be hard-pressed to come up with anyone I wouldn't want here.

Chef Claire and my mother had put together an amazing menu. Until the main course arrived, I was taking full advantage of the appetizer platter sitting directly in front of me. I nodded my approval at Chef Claire and stared down at my plate trying to decide where to start.

The dinner had been a long time coming, and despite the nagging brain-itch of *Who Killed Charlie?,* I was in a terrific mood and finally experiencing an adrenaline rush I could enjoy. I squeezed Max's hand under the table. He patted my thigh and leaned in close for a kiss.

"I'm glad you made it back safe and sound," I said.

"New York was great," he said. "But it would be a tough place to live."

"So I hear," I said, nuzzling his neck. "Too bad the Yankees lost."

"Yeah, it was great until Jameson hit a moon shot in the 7th. The air kind of went out of the stadium. It was like watching a jet take off."

"I still can't believe he's paid thirty million a year to hit a baseball."

"There aren't more than a handful of people who can do what he does," he said with a shrug. "It doesn't matter what your chosen field is, when you're one of the elites, you're worth a whole lot of money."

"Do you think Geraldine is one of the elites in her field?" I said, toying with my glass of iced tea.

"Suzy, I thought you and your mom had a deal," he said, giving my thigh a gentle squeeze.

"Don't. That tickles," I said, wiggling away with a laugh. "I'm trying to concentrate here. And I'm merely making chitchat."

"Okay, Sherlock, whatever you say," he said, shaking his head. "Yeah, I imagine she's at the top of her field. Or close to it."

"What do you think finding the Red Diamond Dagger would do for her career?" I whispered as I glanced around the table to make sure my mother was preoccupied. She was engrossed in a conversation with Paulie and Rooster and having a great time with it. "I can't help but wonder."

"Okay, I'll play," he said, removing his hand from my leg. He leaned back in his chair and took a sip of wine before continuing. "I think once word got out Geraldine did a deal for something as rare as the dagger, people would be lining up to hire her."

"I thought the same thing," I said.

"It's strange," he said. "When I'm working on a recovery project, I'll sometimes see people wandering around the disaster area who obviously aren't local. They never look like they belong. And they spend most of their time picking through the piles of rubble."

"What are they looking for?"

"Scavenging for items of value. The disaster workers call them The Pariahs. Obviously not a term of endearment."

"Are you trying to draw some sort of parallel to Geraldine?" I said, frowning at him.

"Not really," he said, shaking his head. "It's more of a general reference about the person who killed Charlie. His killer and The Pariahs operate from a different perspective, but I think the concept is the same."

"People looking to hit a home run and alter the arc of their lives," I said, nodding as I made the connection.

"Correct. Searching for the Golden Egg that could produce life-changing results," Max said.

"Life-changing as in a windfall of several million dollars?" I said, hating myself again as I flashed back to my conversations with Billy at the party.

"It would certainly be a good start," he said, nodding his thanks at our server who was making the rounds topping off everyone's wine glass.

I waved the server off with a smile.

"You sure you don't want a glass of wine?" Max said. "It might help you relax."

"No, thanks," I said, kissing his cheek. "I'm going to wait and have a glass with dinner."

"Gotta stay sharp and keep a clear head?" he said, chuckling.

"Yeah, just in case," I said, again nuzzling against him. "I suppose there are always people looking for a way to make a killing, pardon the pun, with one quick score."

"There certainly are," he said, nodding. "I blame Indiana Jones."

"You do, do you?" I said, laughing.

"Yes, I do," he said, taking another sip. "Him and Spielberg."

Max turned serious then gently reached out and held my hand on top of the table as he stared at me.

"The thought she or Billy might have killed their father is really gnawing at you, isn't it?"

"Finally, someone understands," I said, forcing a small laugh. "I can't get the thought out of my head. And I hate myself for thinking it."

"As long as it stays a thought, you'll be fine," Max said. "But try not to walk around talking about it. I doubt if anything good could come of it."

"I'm afraid it's a little late," I said, flashing back to the previous evening when I'd managed to annoy Geraldine and make Chef Claire and Josie mad at the same time, something I don't think I'd ever done before. "I'd like to believe someone else did it, especially Charlie's brothers. I really don't like either one of them. But I'm not sure they're smart enough to pull it off."

"It doesn't take a lot of brains to kill somebody," Max said, tossing back what was left of his wine. "But it does take some degree of intelligence to get away with it."

"Oh, so you're going philosophical on me tonight?" I said, laughing.

"You like that one, huh?"

"I do," I said, squeezing his hand. "I can't wait for tomorrow."

"Me either," he said. "I can't wait to be married to you."

"It's going to be amazing. I love you, Max."

"Love you too," he said, getting up from his seat. "If you'll excuse me for a minute, I need to make room for some more wine."

"Do you need help finding the men's room?" I said, turning coy.

"No, I think I know where the bathroom is," he said, flirting back. "I've only been here about a hundred times."

I watched him stroll off, pausing to say hi to some of our guests and accept their congratulations and best wishes. Then I flinched and stared at the far wall of the restaurant with a blank stare. Fortunately, my mother didn't notice. If she had, she would have immediately plopped herself down in Max's chair for a little chat I was sure would be punctuated with several *young lady* references.

But the Chief did see it, and he frowned at me until we made eye contact. I nodded for him to follow me. I excused myself from the table and headed for the bar. I waved to Millie who was frantically trying to keep up with the drink orders coming from the dining room. Apparently, our guests had arrived thirsty. I gave her a wave, and she managed a brief nod before getting back to work. I took a seat on one of the couches near the fireplace. The Chief sat down across from me and studied my face.

"Okay, Snoopmeister," he said, draping a leg over his knee. "Spill it."

I did.

It took me several minutes to outline my theory to him. I occasionally paused to restate some of my ideas. He asked several questions along the way to help me clarify my thinking as well as his own understanding. When I finished, I sat back on the couch and waited for his response. Eventually, he nodded.

"I can make it work," he said. "How do you feel about it?"

"I'm not sure. It seems like a bit of a stretch," I said, shrugging. "But it's better than anything else we've come up with."

"It is," the Chief said. "But there is one problem."

"The one about how to get the killer to tip their hand?"

"Yeah," he said. "You got any ideas how we're going to do it?"

"As a matter of fact, I do," I said, nodding. "I thought we'd start by offering to set up a meeting to hand over the dagger for a cut of the proceeds."

"Pure, simple greed. Always a good place to start. And when do you propose on having this meeting?"

"I thought we'd do it at the reception," I said, unable to make eye contact.

"What?" he said, stunned. "Are you out of your mind, Suzy? You want to try to smoke out Charlie's killer at your wedding reception?"

"When else are we going to do it?" I said, shrugging. "People are going to start leaving town as soon as the reception is over. Or the next morning."

"I can't believe we're having this conversation," he said. "No, absolutely not."

"C'mon, Chief," I said. "It won't take more than a few minutes. We'll get it done, and I'll be back in my seat before the next toast. And you'll have all sorts of cops hanging around. Tell you what, we'll do it late. After we cut the cake and get through the first dance."

"How about you let me handle it?" he said.

"It won't work, Chief," I said. "It can't be a cop making the first move. If it's me, there's a good chance I can get the conversation jumpstarted. You know the effect I have on people."

"Yeah, I could probably ballpark it," he deadpanned.

"Funny," I said. "What do you say?"

"I say no," he snapped. "What happened to the promise you made to your mother?"

"Nothing happened to it," I said with a shrug. "Technically, I promised my mother I wouldn't do any snooping until after the wedding. Unless I'm mistaken, the reception comes *after* the wedding."

"I doubt if your mother is going to make the distinction," Chief Abrams said.

"Oh, I'm sure she won't. And it's why we're not going to tell her. She's got enough to worry about."

"What are you going to do when she finds out?" he said.

"I'll be on a boat heading downriver by then. She'll have more than enough time to cool off while we're on our honeymoon. And I have something else up my sleeve that's going to help."

"It better be good," he said. "Because she is going to go ballistic."

"She'll be fine," I said. "I'll be able to keep her preoccupied."

"I really don't like this idea, Suzy," the Chief said.

"It's only going to be a conversation, Chief," I said. "Followed by the arrival of several cops carrying guns."

"What's your plan for getting the killer to show up without revealing who you are?"

"I thought we'd slide a note under the door," I said, beaming at him.

"A note under the door?"

"Yeah, a phone call isn't a good idea. Neither one of us wants our voice recognized," I said. "And I like the low-tech nature of the old note under the door."

"Do you now?" he said, getting to his feet. "Okay, we need to get back. The toasts are about to start, and it would be a great idea for the bride to be there when they do."

"Cool," I said, also standing up and cocking my arm for him to slide his in. "Kind sir, if you would do me the honor of escorting me back to my seat."

"Unbelievable," he said, exhaling loudly. "Okay, I'll give it some thought. But we'll be talking about this again at some point tomorrow."

"Really, Chief? On my wedding day?" I said with mock surprise.

"Don't start, young lady."

Chapter 17

My wedding day began, as I'd always hoped it would, with a glorious sunrise that seemed to set the River on fire. And when the early morning daylight blossomed, various shades of green set against the backdrop of a deep-blue sky put a smile on my face that refused to leave. But despite the significance of my special day, our standard house rule still applied: The first one up makes the coffee and lets the dogs out for their morning pee. I did both, then again stared out the kitchen window listening to the sounds of boat engines making their way to deep water.

"Happy Wedding Day," Josie said as she entered the kitchen and gave me a long hug. "Did you get any sleep?"

"I slept great," I said, impatiently waiting for the coffeemaker to stop gurgling. "But it was a bit strange. It's the first time I've slept alone in quite a while."

"Well, you know the rules," she said, opening the kitchen door to let the dogs back in. "Good morning, bruisers." She knelt to say hello to all four dogs, then sat down at the kitchen island. "The groom can't see the bride before the ceremony. It's bad luck."

I sat down on the floor with my legs splayed. The dogs took full advantage. They all vied for attention, and I did my best to

170

return their affection before getting to my feet to pour the coffee. Chef Claire entered the kitchen in her robe, yawning.

"Good morning," she said, bending down to say hi to the dogs. Eventually, she was able to make her way to the island and sat down next to Josie. "It's beautiful outside. What do you guys feel like doing today?" she deadpanned.

"Funny," I said, setting steaming mugs of coffee in front of both of them. Then a wave of melancholy washed over me. "This is the last morning we're ever going to do this."

"I seriously doubt it," Josie said, then took a sip.

"You know what I mean," I said, shrugging. "The last time we'll do it as roommates."

"Tell you what," Josie said. "You have our permission to cook breakfast for us anytime you like."

"You're not helping," I said, making a face at her.

"This is a day for happiness," she said. "Save the melancholy for another time."

"Like late at night after we've all had too much wine," Chef Claire said.

"There you go," Josie said, raising her mug in salute.

"It's going to be weird," I said.

"It's going to be fine," Chef Claire said, then reached for a jar of dog biscuits. She tossed one to each dog who were sitting on their haunches next to the counter. They all expertly snatched them out of the air. Chef Claire repeated the process. "What time do we need to be at the church?"

171

"Ten-thirty," Josie said, glancing down at the set of instructions my mother had dropped off yesterday.

We'd been over the schedule a dozen times, and I was sure it was ingrained. But my mother wasn't taking any chances.

"Your mom wants us fully dressed and ready to go by 10:15. The ceremony starts at eleven, followed by a photo session in the garden behind the church. Then we'll head to the reception."

"It's going to be hot," Chef Claire said. "Why did she insist on doing it in the middle of the day?"

"For the lighting," I said, shaking my head. "She wants midday sun when the photographer starts doing his thing."

"We got lucky with the weather," Chef Claire said as she glanced out the window.

"Luck had nothing to do with it," I said. "It wouldn't dare rain today. My mother would never forgive Him."

Josie and Chef Claire laughed. Josie got up to refill our mugs then sat back down. Then something caught her attention outside.

"Here comes the floor show," she said, heading for the kitchen door.

"Let me guess," I said, glancing out at the driveway.

I got up and grabbed another mug from a cabinet, poured, then added a splash of milk. Josie opened the door and my mother entered. Queen, her King Charles spaniel, was tucked under one arm, and she gently set her down on the floor. Our house dogs greeted her and soon Captain was rolling around with her on the floor. The others joined in, and the kitchen was soon filled with playful growls and thrashing legs.

"Okay, guys," Josie said, her voice lowered as she gave them a straightforward command. "Living room."

All five trotted off. Peace and quiet returned.

"You're up early, Mom," I said, returning the long hug she gave me.

"Oh, I've been up for hours," she said, sitting down next to Chef Claire. "And I wanted to make sure you weren't sleeping in."

"No, we're right on schedule."

"Good," she said, taking a sip of coffee. "But don't get cocky. We've got a long day ahead of us."

"Got it, Sarge," I said, grinning at her.

"Save your witty banter for the reception, darling," she said. "How do you plan to handle the house dogs today? It's going to be hot. And the last thing I need is to be worrying about Queen."

"We're going to put them out on the verandah and leave the gate open," Josie said. "They'll be able to come and go as they please. And we're leaving several bowls of water. They'll be fine."

"It wouldn't even be a question if you'd let me incorporate them into the wedding," I said, unable to resist broaching the subject again.

"Darling, you're getting married in a Catholic church," my mother said, shaking her head. "There was no way Father Phillips was ever going to agree to let four dogs walk down the aisle with you."

"It would have been adorable," I said, shrugging. "Chloe would have made a great ring bearer. And Chef Claire had already taught Al and Dente to carry baskets of rose petals."

"I'm sure it will come in handy at some point," my mother said, taking another sip. "And what was Captain's job going to be?"

"Security," Josie deadpanned.

"Well, I'm sorry to have disappointed you, darling. As much as I love your dogs, that one was not open for debate. You're sure you wouldn't like to bring them to the reception for a while?"

All three of us shook our heads.

"No way," Josie said. "Way too many people wanting to feed them. And as delicious as I'm sure the food is going to be, we're serving some things they can't eat."

"Of course. You're right," my mother said, then spoke to Josie and Chef Claire. "Is it okay if I pick Queen up tomorrow morning?"

"Absolutely, Mrs. C.," Chef Claire said.

My mother finished her coffee then stood and gave me another long hug. She let go but continued to hold my shoulders with both hands as she stared at my face.

174

"What is it?" I said, frowning.

"Just checking to make sure you're perfect," she said, beaming at me. "Well done, darling. Mission accomplished."

"Thanks, Mom," I said, blushing.

"Are you nervous?"

"Not yet. But the day is young."

"You'll be fine," she said, letting go and strolling toward the door. "But make sure you remember all your lines."

"I'll do my best."

"The limo will be here at 10:20," she said, glancing around at all three of us to reinforce her point. "Please try to be ready."

"We will, Mom."

"Have you packed for the honeymoon?"

"I have."

"Lots of silk and frills, right?"

"None of your business, Mom."

"Harsh. Got your passport and tickets?"

"Yup."

"Yup?" she said, rolling her eyes at me. "Try again, darling."

"What?"

"I said try again."

It finally dawned on me what she was doing, and I grinned at her.

"Okay, Mom. I'll play."

"You always were a quick study," she said, again beaming at me. "Do you have a change of clothes for the reception?"

"I do."

"Well done, darling," she said, giving us a finger wave as she headed out the door. "But make sure you speak up. I want everyone in the church to hear you."

I waited until the door closed behind her and turned to Josie and Chef Claire.

"Why do I have the feeling this is going to be a very long day?"

"I doubt she'll ever admit it, but she's nervous," Josie said, washing the coffee mugs. "It's the biggest day she's had in a long time. And she's been waiting for this one forever."

"I suppose you're right," I said.

"And I'm sure she's missing your dad today," Chef Claire said.

"Yeah," I whispered. "She's not the only one."

I felt myself tearing up, and I exhaled loudly. Right on cue, both of my best friends gave me a long hug, and it continued until they were sure the wave of emotion surging through me had passed.

"Whew," I said, shaking my head. "Where the heck did that come from?"

"I'm sure it won't be the last one today," Josie said. "But don't worry, we're here. So whatever you need, ask."

"The first thing I'm going to need is some help getting my dress zipped up."

Chapter 18

After a long, hot shower, I applied tons of lotion, a generous dash of baby powder then dried my hair. Millie and Jill, the other members of my bridal party, had offered to do my hair. I did my best to sit still as they worked their magic. When they finished, I nodded in the mirror and thanked them profusely. I was wearing it up and loved the way it looked. It certainly wasn't how I'd wear it around the Inn when I was working, or even close to the way I tied it back in a ponytail stuffed inside a baseball cap when I was out on the River. But for today it was perfect. Millie and Jill headed down the hall to shower and change. I slipped out of my towel and began to get dressed.

When I was ready, I stepped into my wedding dress, a gorgeous gown my mother and I had picked out during a shopping trip to Montreal and turned around to look at myself in the mirror. Then I reached behind my back for the zipper and quickly gave it up as a lost cause. I whistled loudly once. Moments later all five dogs came trotting into my bedroom. They sat down and stared up at me with their heads cocked.

"I'm sorry, guys," I said, laughing. "It's sweet of you to offer, but I'm afraid I'm going to need opposable thumbs for this one."

Chef Claire poked her head through the door.

"You bellowed?" she said, shooing the dogs out as she came in and closed the door behind her.

"Yeah, I need some help with this zipper," I said, again staring into the mirror.

"Your hair looks great," she said, reaching behind me. "Take a deep breath and hold it."

I did and heard the sound of the zipper as it raced up my back.

"Okay, you can exhale now," she said, gently turning me around by the shoulders to get a good look. "You look beautiful."

"Thanks."

"How does the dress feel?"

"Pretty good," I said. "Mind you, it's not as comfortable as shorts and a tee shirt, but what are you gonna do, right?"

"Yeah, the sacrifices we make," she said, laughing. "Max is a very lucky man. And don't ever let him forget it."

"Thanks, Chef Claire," I said, giving her a quick hug.

Josie, looking resplendent in her maid of honor dress, knocked gently then opened the door. She entered and stood in the doorway giving me the once-over. Then she frowned at me.

"What's the matter?" I said.

"That's what you're wearing?" Josie deadpanned.

Chef Claire snorted, and I made a face at her.

"Funny."

"I've been working on my material for a long time," Josie said with a big grin. "Wait until you hear my toast."

"Thanks for the warning," I said. "Okay, I think I'm ready."

"You look stunning," Josie said, pulling me in close for a long embrace. "I'm so happy for you, Suzy."

"Me too," Chef Claire said, tearing up.

"Oh, I almost forgot," I said, heading for one of my dresser drawers. "Give Millie and Jill a shout."

Chef Claire headed out and soon returned with the other two in tow. I reached into the drawer and removed four identical, gift-wrapped boxes.

"I got these for you as a special thank you," I said, handing them out. "And I couldn't resist getting one for myself and my mom. I thought we'd all wear them today."

They each unwrapped their gift. Jill spotted what was inside the box first.

"Holy crap," she whispered as she held the necklace up with both hands.

"They're nothing like the Red Diamond dagger, but I thought they were cute."

"Don't start," Chef Claire said, her voice rising a notch. "We had a deal. No murder talk today."

"Sorry," I said, chastised.

"Geez, Suzy," Josie said, shaking her head. "You didn't need to do this."

"It was the least I could do," I said, glancing around at them.

"These must have cost a fortune," Chef Claire said, turning the necklace over in her hands.

"It's too much," Josie said, shaking her head.

"You want me to take it back?" I deadpanned.

"Over my dead body," Josie said, laughing. "Thank you, Suzy. It's beautiful."

"You're very welcome. All of you. Thanks again for agreeing to stand up with me today."

"This is amazing," Millie said as she and Jill took turns fastening each other's necklaces.

"Maybe we should rethink the idea of Captain handling security," Josie said, admiring her necklace in the mirror. Then she gave me another long hug. "What are we gonna do with you?"

"Well, at the moment, you need to help me get into the limo," I said, glancing at my watch.

"I'll meet you at the car," Josie said. "I'm going to put the dogs out on the verandah and make sure they're good to go."

The rest of us made our way out of the house and slowly walked down the driveway where a white limo was waiting with the backdoors open. Before I climbed in, I took one final look up at the house. It would be the last time I'd see it for a few weeks. It was also the last time I'd see it with Josie and Chef Claire as my roommates. But the excitement of finally being married to

Max pushed away all my concerns. I settled into the backseat with a contented smile.

Minutes later, we arrived at the church and our driver parked in back. We slipped unseen through a side door and Rooster, looking very dashing in a black tux, greeted us immediately.

"Wow," he said, glancing around at us as he shook his head. "Oh, what I'd give to be twenty again."

"Aren't you sweet," Chef Claire said as she bussed his cheek.

"You look so beautiful, Suzy," he said, giving me a hug but being careful not to smear my makeup or mess up my dress.

"Thanks, Rooster."

"C'mon, let's get you guys out of sight," he said, pointing at a nearby door. "The AC is on in there so you should be fine. And your mom left a bottle of champagne in case any of you wanted to settle your nerves before the ceremony."

He escorted us inside the room then told us he'd be back at eleven sharp. Not wanting to wrinkle our outfits, we remained standing or sitting on the edge of the couch while Josie poured champagne for all of us. I accepted the glass and waited for the toast I knew was coming.

"To Suzy and Max," Josie said, raising her glass. "May your life together be as good as the one you've both lived up to this point."

"To Suzy and Max," the others repeated.

We clinked glasses, and I took a small sip then set my glass down. I felt completely at peace as I checked my watch. Fifteen minutes to showtime. We heard a soft knock and my mother entered.

"Well done, ladies. You all look gorgeous," she said, glancing around. "I'm glad to see you're enjoying the champagne. Don't drink too much, darling. I don't want you staggering down the aisle."

"Got it, Mom," I said, then took a good look at her outfit and the necklace she was wearing. "You look fabulous."

"Thank you, darling," she said. "I was about to say the same thing to you. Could I have a quiet word with you?"

"Sure," I said, following her to the back corner of the room. "What's up?"

She smiled at me as she brushed an imaginary wrinkle from my dress and continued to fuss over me and my outfit. I was about to swat her hand away when she stopped and gently held me by the shoulders.

"I want to tell you how incredibly proud I am of you, darling," she said, tearing up.

"You're gonna make me cry, Mom."

"Better here than out there," she said, dabbing her eyes with a tissue. "I know I don't tell you enough how much I love you. And it's something I plan on rectifying in the future."

"Don't start doing anything crazy, Mom," I said, reaching for one of her tissues.

"Hush," she said, laughing. "I only wish your father could be here today."

"He's here," I said, then a thought popped. I grinned at her. "Although now that I think about it, he never did enjoy going to church."

"No, he didn't, did he?" she said, shaking her head. "It was like pulling teeth getting him here. You two always preferred being out on the River."

"As did you, Mom."

"Yes, but someone needed to set an example," she said, squeezing my hand. "Okay, I think it's almost showtime. Dazzle them, darling."

"I'll do my best, Mom," I said, pulling her close. "Thanks for everything you've done to make this day special."

"I was about to say the same thing to you. I love you so much."

"I love you too, Mom."

Then the tears started flowing. It took us a couple of minutes to compose ourselves then we wiped each other eyes and exhaled loudly. My mother wheeled around and headed back to where the rest of the bridal party were doing their best not to eavesdrop.

"Ladies, I'd like to thank you again," she said. "You all look magnificent."

"Thanks, Mrs. C.," Chef Claire said, gently placing a hand on my mother's arm.

184

"Great dress," Josie said.

"This old thing?" my mother said with a coy smile. "Millie, I got a look at the groomsman who's going to be walking down the aisle with you. He's gorgeous. And from what I hear, quite single at the moment."

"Are you playing matchmaker, Mrs. C.?" Millie said with a grin.

"Have fun, Millie," I said, laughing.

My mother flashed me *the look*.

"We just had a wonderful moment, darling. Try not to ruin it."

"I'll see what I can do, Mom," I said with a laugh.

"Okay, stay sharp. But have fun. And I'll need all of you in the back garden for photos as soon as we finish the receiving line after the ceremony. Try not to dawdle."

She exited with a wave.

"She looks great," Josie said.

"She's my hero," Chef Claire said.

"Yeah, you could do a lot worse," I said, then glanced down at my watch.

Two minutes to eleven.

I felt my insides begin to churn, and I fought back the grimace beginning to form. I pressed a hand against my stomach.

"Are you okay?" Josie said.

"I'm fine," I said. "My stomach is rumbling a bit."

"Perfectly understandable," she said, reaching into her purse. She pulled out a bag of bite-sized and held it out.

"Good call," I said, taking two.

"But you better get them down in a hurry. If you walk down the aisle with chocolate on your face, she's gonna blame me."

Chapter 19

I took my place next to Rooster at the back of the procession. He gently squeezed my hand and gave me a quick once-over.

"You look beautiful," he whispered.

"You're looking sharp yourself, Rooster."

"I clean up pretty well when I make an effort. How are you holding up?"

"I'm a lot more nervous than I expected."

"Five hundred pairs of eyes focused on you? Why would that make you nervous?"

"You're not helping."

"Focus on your breathing."

I did.

"Hey, how about that? It works," I said, leaning in to give him a peck on the cheek.

"I smell chocolate," he said. "I went with Jack Daniels, but that's just me."

I laughed and squeezed his arm.

"Thanks again for agreeing to give me away, Rooster."

"No problem," he said. "I wanted to sell you, but your mom wouldn't let me."

That got a laugh from everyone in the bridal party. I glanced around to make sure my mother was out of earshot then took a few more deep breaths. The organist launched into *Here Comes the Bride*. Josie glanced at me over her shoulder.

"Last chance," she deadpanned. "We can be in Canada in ten minutes."

"Eyes front," I said, gently punching her on the shoulder.

Then the procession began to move. Rooster held me right where I was until Josie was twenty feet ahead of us. From the back of the church, I watched Millie and Jill, both accompanied by groomsmen, slowly make their way toward the altar. In the distance, I saw Max and his brother, the best man, already in place and staring at the back of the church. Josie continued her slow, long walk down the aisle. Rooster offered his arm, and I hooked mine under it.

"You're gonna do great," he whispered.

The bite-sized hadn't done the trick, and my stomach churned and rumbled as we began our walk. Along the way, I made eye contact with dozens of people I knew and a surge of memories flooded through me. They helped take my mind off what seemed to be an endless trek through the rows of pews.

"I think it was a good call not to do a full mass," I whispered.

"Yeah, this heat is brutal," he whispered, sweat already beading up on his forehead. He sensed the wobbly nature of my knees. "Hang in there. We'll be at the reception before you know it."

"These shoes are killing me."

"You want me to carry you?"

I stifled a snort and squeezed his hand.

"Can you imagine the look on her face?"

Twenty feet from the altar I got my first good look at Max who was beaming at me. I made the last few steps without incident and Max winked at me and reached out his hand to help me up the marble steps. Rooster nodded to Father Adams, our local priest, then took a seat next to my mother.

With round one complete, I took a few more deep breaths and beamed at Max.

"You look amazing," he whispered.

"Thanks. You look great in a tux. Maybe you should wear it more often."

"Not a chance," he said.

"No kidding," I said, fighting off a foot cramp and doing my best to ignore the trail of sweat tickling my spine on the way down. "My feet are killing me."

"Mine too," Max said. "And these shoes are really slippery. I almost broke my neck coming up the steps."

"Oh, let's not go there," I said with a giggle. "It would put a damper on the day."

Father Adams glanced back and forth at us with a patient smile, then looked around the packed church and addressed the throng. A few minutes into his opening prayers and welcoming remarks, my nerves began to settle a bit, and I spotted the best man and groomsmen sneaking furtive glances at Josie and the rest of the bridal party. Before I knew it, it was time for us to exchange vows. Father Adams beamed at us. Receiving no response from either of us and sensing our nervousness, he leaned in close.

"If you would face each other and hold hands, please," he whispered. "Just like we did it in rehearsal."

"Sure, sure."

"Please repeat after me," Father Adams said to Max. "I Max."

"I Max."

"Take you, Suzy, to be my lawful wedded wife."

"Take you, Suzy, to be my lawful wedded wife," Max repeated in a loud voice.

"To have and to hold, from this day forward, for better, for worse, for richer, for poorer, in sickness and in health, until death do us part."

"To have and to hold," Max said, starting slowly. Then his memory kicked in. "From this day forward, for better, for worse, for richer, for poorer, in sickness and in health-"

In an attempt to look directly into my eyes, Max shuffled his feet to get closer to me. But his foot slipped on the marble and he lost his balance. He windmilled his arms to catch himself before toppling off the top step. He bounced down the short set of steps and ended up splayed out on the floor in front of the altar.

"Oh, crap," I said, scrambling down the steps. I knelt over him, and he stared up at me with a glazed stare. "Are you all right?"

Despite their best efforts, several people in the audience snorted and laughed. I suppose at some point I'll look back and find the humor in it, but this wasn't the time.

"Yeah, I'm fine," he said, climbing to his feet and brushing himself off. "I'm a total idiot."

I held his arm as he limped his way back in place. He wobbled briefly before finding his balance.

"Told you he'd fall at some point," the best man whispered to the groomsman standing next to him. "You owe me twenty bucks."

Josie gave him the death stare, and his face flushed bright red.

"Where was I?" Max said, glancing back and forth at Father Adams and me.

"You were at the until death do us part," I said.

"Oh, right. Until death do us part."

"Smooth," I whispered, stifling a chuckle.

I repeated my vows without incident then Father Adams addressed the crowd. He did a short call and response, recited a prayer, and said the magic words.

"By the power vested in me, I now pronounce you husband and wife."

Just like that, it was over. The crowd burst into loud applause and Max and I turned to beam and wave at everyone. I caught my mother's eye, and she had a massive grin with tears streaming down her face. I choked back my emotions, returned her small wave and the two thumbs up Rooster was giving me. We slowly made our way down the steps with me keeping a close eye out for obstacles Max might trip over until we were on level ground. The walk back down the aisle was much easier, and we were soon standing outside on the front steps.

"It wasn't too bad," Max said, rubbing his knee.

"Are you sure you're okay? You took quite a tumble."

"Nothing a couple of cocktails won't fix."

"It's gonna be a while," I said. "Receiving line, then photos."

On cue, my mother appeared and began organizing us in a line on the front lawn. It took a long time to greet everyone and thank them for coming. I thought I was going to wilt in the heat, but it was only the prequel to the photo session. By the time we were finally finished, we'd gone through several bottles of cold water and countless makeup retouches the photographer's assistant was desperately trying to keep up with. Mercifully, it ended after an hour, and we piled into the back of two airconditioned limos to make the short drive to my mom's place.

"I can't wait to get out of this dress," I said, dabbing at the sweat covering my face and neck.

"I'll be happy to give you a hand," Max said, raising his pant leg to reveal a large bruise below his left knee.

"Geez," I said, staring at it. "Nasty."

"Can I use it as an excuse not to dance?"

"Not a chance," I said, laughing.

When we arrived at my mother's place, we all climbed out of the limos and made our way to the edge of the backyard next to the house. The lawn had been transformed into a massive tented enclosure, and a stage had been constructed on one side. Onstage, a piano player I didn't know was playing jazz. He wasn't as proficient as Summerman, few people were, but he was good, and the crowd was enjoying him. I had no idea where my mother had found him on short notice, but she'd made a good choice. All the guests were in full-party mode, sipping cocktails and sampling a wide variety of appetizers on silver trays the servers were offering. A constant hum of conversation and laughter filled the yard, accented by the soft whir of fans ringing the area; a last-ditch effort on my mother's part to keep the oppressive air circulating.

My feet ached, and I removed my shoes.

"Ahh," I sighed as my feet sunk into the thick, cool grass.

"Great idea," Chef Claire said as she kicked her shoes off.

Josie did the same then collected all three pairs of shoes and tossed them on the back porch. I spotted my mother talking with

193

a group of friends. She was, for lack of a better word, ebullient and when she spotted us standing at the far end of the lawn, she waved and motioned for us to *make the walk.*

My mother and I had several heated conversations while putting together the wedding plans. Twice our conversations had boiled over into full-blown arguments leaving both of us sullen and bawling our eyes out. Fortunately, we quickly apologized to each other and moved on until the next *point of discussion* raised its ugly head. One of the more challenging debates arose one night during a family dinner at our house when my mother raised the question of how we wanted to be introduced upon our arrival at the reception. When Max and I stated firmly we didn't want an introduction, my mother's eyes narrowed. She glanced back and forth at us as if we had announced our intention to join ISIS.

It was the first time Max had witnessed firsthand my mother's dark side, and I heard him gulp.

"It's essential you don't show any fear," I'd whispered to him. "If you do, we're toast."

"Why on earth wouldn't you want to be introduced as a new couple, darling?"

She'd used *darling* instead of *young lady* so I knew I had some time to talk her through it before she blew a gasket.

"Because we don't need an introduction, Mom," I said with a shrug. "And we both think having a guy with a microphone announcing, *ladies and gentlemen, for the first time ever*, blah, blah, blah is, well, corny."

"Corny?" she said. "I see." She fixed a hard stare on Max. "Did she talk you into this, or is this how you really feel, Max?"

"It is," he said after I'd dug my fingernails into his thigh.

The debate continued for several minutes, but we hung tough. The impasse was finally broken when Josie who'd been listening quietly leaned forward to address the table.

"It's none of my business," she said. "But one question does come to mind. If some of the guests need an introduction or be reminded Suzy and Max are officially married, I can't help but wonder why those people were invited to the wedding in the first place."

My mother visibly flinched and had no immediate retort ready. I would have given Josie a high-five, but it would have been rubbing it in. My mother withdrew her objections, and it was decided Max and I would stroll across the lawn, hand in hand, and deal with whatever spontaneous reaction we received.

The memory faded and I came back to the moment. I glanced at Max who was standing next to me.

"Are you ready to do this?"

"I am," he said, taking my hand. "Lead the way."

"Watch your step," I deadpanned. "The grass can get slippery."

"Funny," he said, squeezing my hand.

We started walking across the lawn and were soon greeted by a standing ovation. Both our faces flushed red with embarrassment as we nodded and acknowledged the applause.

We came to a stop next to my mother. She gave Max a long embrace and a kiss on the cheek.

"My son-in-law," she said, staring into his eyes. "It sounds so good. It's like music to my ears."

"I'm the lucky one," Max said.

"You were right, darling," she said as she pulled me in close for a hug. "Spontaneous was definitely the way to go."

"Score one for Suzy," I said, then looked at Max. "Write it down in case I forget."

"Save your wit for the toasts, darling."

"Where are we on the schedule, Mom?"

"We're going to eat in twenty minutes," she said, checking her watch. "Then we'll cut the cake, make the toasts, and do the other handful of traditions you finally agreed to. Then it's the first dance."

"Then we'll be free?" I said, raising an eyebrow at her.

"Geez, darling. You'd think you were waiting to be released into the wild."

"Just checking, Mom," I said, giving her another hug.

Max spotted his brother and his groomsmen standing nearby.

"I need to have a chat with my brother about his toast. I don't trust him as far as I can throw him," Max said with a laugh. "But I think we'll do it over a cold beer. Can I get you something?"

"No, I'm good. I'm going to mingle a bit. I'll see you at the head table."

"It's a date," he said, limping off.

Josie and Chef Claire, along with Millie and Jill, finished their trek across the lawn and all four gave me long, sweaty hugs.

"Wonderful job, ladies," my mother said.

"Thanks, Mrs. C.," Jill said. "She makes a beautiful bride, doesn't she?"

"She certainly does," my mother said, beaming at me.

"Are you sure he's okay?" Chef Claire said, staring at Max as he continued his slow limp toward his best man.

"Yeah, he'll be fine," I said. "But it was quite a tumble."

"It was certainly something you don't see at most weddings," Josie said. "I need a drink."

"I'll join you in a few minutes," Chef Claire said. "I want to check to make sure everything is ready to go with dinner."

"Chef Claire, you're not working today," my mother said. "If there is a problem, let me handle it."

"Don't worry about it, Mrs. C. I won't be long," she said, waving as she strolled off.

"She never stops, does she?" my mother said.

"She will," Josie said. "Right after I get a couple of glasses of champagne in her. Can I get you a glass?"

"I think I'm going to start with a club soda," I said. "This heat is brutal."

Chapter 20

My mother's welcome speech, was a five-minute combination of introductions, thanks, and two tributes. One tribute was to Charlie Merrihew. It produced a lengthy, unrequested moment of silence throughout the crowd. Her other tribute was to me and Max, a concise, affectionate set of comments she delivered effortlessly. As soon as she sat down to a big round of applause, dinner was served. It was a delicious three-course feast - two for me since I waved off the server when he tried to set a piece of grilled salmon bathing in a dill-lemon-butter sauce in front of me. The food had the crowd murmuring in appreciation. I leaned forward to thank Chef Claire who was sitting a few seats away from me. She grinned and raised her glass in salute.

Breaking with another tradition, we had decided to postpone our first dance until after we had cut the cake. Max and I thought, and my mother had quickly agreed, when the piano music ended, and the band finally started playing, it would serve as notice to our guests the formal part of the day was over, and the real party was about to begin. We also thought the flow of the day would be improved by making the minor tweaks to the traditional order.

But before we could cut the cake, we had a round of toasts to get through. Max's brother went first and produced several rounds of belly laughs when he recounted several incidents during my husband's childhood when his accident-prone nature had caused serious damage to his physical well-being. According to his brother, Max had fallen out of a tree twice, fallen through thin ice, tripped over curbs, rocks, family dogs, and, one time, even his own mother. He finished his speech to loud applause then handed the microphone to Josie. She stood and glanced around the crowd before starting.

"That was an impressive list," she said, shaking her head as she grinned at the best man. "But you failed to mention one other fall Max has taken. And, no, I'm not talking about the tumble at the church earlier today." She paused until the laughter died down. "I'm talking about the time when Max *fell* madly in love with my best friend, Suzy." She waited out a round of oohs and aahs. "Yeah, it was a sweet comment. But since sweet really isn't my style, let me tell you the other side of the story." She gave me an evil smile, and I shook my head as I prepared myself for the worst. "For those of you who don't know, Max isn't the only one who is, shall we say, a bit challenged in the klutz factor."

"Crap," I whispered, knowing exactly where she was going with her speech.

Josie began to regale the audience with several examples of how I'd managed to do some serious damage to myself. She

199

started with the time when I had gotten a severe sunburn on my butt in the Cayman Islands and how the loose-fitting shorts I was wearing to minimize chafing, had ended up around my ankles with me face down on the floor of Gerald's office just as his personal assistant had entered. Gerald, the Premier, was in the crowd sitting at my mother's table and he laughed louder than anybody.

"It's burned into my memory," Gerald called out.

"You mooned the Cayman Premier?" Max whispered as he leaned in close.

"Long story," I said, shrugging.

Josie followed it up one with another Cayman story; this one about the time when we'd been diving with the stingrays and one of them had sliced through the string holding my bikini top up. This was soon followed by the stingray latching onto one of my breasts and leaving a mark that looked exactly like a hickey. Josie had to pause for almost a minute until the laughter died down. Then she looked over at me.

"Should I go on?" she asked coyly.

"Knock yourself out," I said, managing a laugh as I held up my left hand and flashed my wedding ring. "He's not going anywhere now."

"Let's see, what else?" she said, holding a finger to her chin. "There's just so many choices. I guess I could mention the time she had the *brilliant* idea for us to kidnap a bunch of roosters from an illegal cockfight. Another Cayman story in case you were wondering. And with Gerald's help, we were somehow able to avoid jail and deportation." She paused to take a sip of champagne. "But let's move closer to home, shall we?"

She continued her relentless narration of my exploits including the time in Ottawa I'd gotten trapped outside on the balcony of a downtown loft during a major snowstorm wearing only a housekeeping uniform to keep me warm. Max, an eyewitness to the incident, laughed and nodded as Josie retold the story. Other stories about things in and around Clay Bay, Canada, and even Mexico followed. She finally finished with my most recent misadventure in Las Vegas when I'd gotten locked inside a freezer used as a high-end, vodka tasting room. The tale produced the loudest outburst of laughter yet, but she wasn't done. By the time she finished telling the story of how I'd fallen asleep on top of the ice-bar and managed to get the side of my face stuck, an explosion of laughter reverberated back and forth across the tented lawn.

"So, as you can see, Max," Josie said. "You've got your work cut out for you to keep up with your wife. She sets a pretty high bar. But from what I saw at the church today, I think you've got a real shot."

Josie paused again to wait out another round of laughter and take another sip of champagne. Then she turned serious, and her voice softened.

"But what you all need to understand about Suzy is she gets herself into these situations in one of two ways. The first is when she is doing everything she can to rectify an injustice being done to people, many of whom she has never even met. The second is to assist, rescue, or save animals from cruel sometimes even inhumane treatment at the hands of despicable people. And even when she makes me mad enough to kick her in the butt repeatedly, she remains steadfast in both pursuits."

Tears were now streaming down both our faces.

"She is fearless and the most intuitive person I've ever met, is generous to a fault, and someone I would run through fire for. But knowing Suzy, she's probably the one who managed to start it." Josie waited out a short burst of laughter before continuing. "I am proud to call her my business partner. More importantly, I am honored to call her my friend. My best friend in the whole world." She raised her glass to me then looked at Max. "I know you understand how lucky you are, Max. And I couldn't be happier you two found each other. I also know you will do everything you can to make her happy." She paused one more time to give Max a coy smile. "Because if you don't, Chef Claire and I, if necessary, will hunt you down to the far corners of the earth."

Max laughed and nodded. Josie raised her glass high and addressed the crowd.

"To the happy couple."

"To the happy couple," the crowd repeated.

Josie finished to a standing ovation, and she gave me a long hug on the way back to her seat.

"I'm gonna kill you," I whispered into her ear with a laugh.

"You'll have to catch me first," she whispered back and squeezed me even tighter.

"Thank you."

"No, thank you."

"I love you."

"I love you too."

Chapter 21

Reggie Cullen was a lifelong friend I'd known since I'd started walking. An enormously talented artist, as well as an accomplished musician, he and three other friends had formed a band when they hit their teenage years. And soon, the Midnight Ryders were playing at all our high school dances and various parties. As we got older, they began playing bars and clubs and kept playing. Over the years they'd gotten even tighter, and I had been delighted when my mother suggested them as a replacement for Summerman's band. Their playing at the reception was going to give the party a local feel, and I knew they'd quickly get people dancing and keep them on their feet.

After I wolfed down my second piece of cake, I excused myself from the table and made my way to the stage where the band was putting the finishing touches on their set up. Reggie spotted me heading his way, and he set his guitar down and walked to the edge of the stage.

"Quite a speech Josie gave," he said, laughing. "Are all those stories about you true?"

"Sadly, yes," I said, shrugging. "I want to thank you for doing this on very short notice."

"We're happy to do it," Reggie said. "But I have to admit we were all looking forward to hearing Summerman's band."

"He said he's gonna make it up to us," I said. "But I really mean it, Reggie. You saved our butt, and I'll never forget it."

"Suzy, stop," he said, waving it off. "We're honored to do it. And since we were already coming to the wedding, it's not like we had anything else going on."

"Still," I said, protesting. "I'm just glad my mother was able to convince you to do it."

"Well, your mother is a little hard to say no to," he said, laughing again. "Especially when she's got her checkbook in her hand."

"She made it worth your while?"

"Oh, yeah," he said with a big grin.

"Good," I said. "Max and I are going to do the first dance in about half an hour. Were you guys able to learn the song?"

"We got you covered," he said, nodding. "I think it's going to work well. How did you and Max come up with it?"

"It's a long story," I said, laughing.

I drifted off as I remembered the debates about what song we would use for our first dance. It must have gone on for quite a while because I flinched when I was brought back to the present by his voice.

"Are you still here?" Reggie said, giving me an odd look.

"Yeah, I'm here. Sorry. I was thinking about a conversation I had with my mom. Look, I need to run. But thanks again, Reggie. I'll see you in a bit."

205

"You got it," he said with a grin, then picked his guitar up to continue tuning it.

I spotted Josie and Chef Claire near one of the bars and headed straight for them.

"I'm going to head inside to grab a quick shower and change my clothes," I said, lifting the neckline of my dress off my skin in a futile attempt to cool off. "I'm sweating like a pig in this dress."

"I'm in," Chef Claire said. "I've been soaked since the ceremony."

"Pigs don't sweat," Josie said, fanning herself.

"Thanks for clarifying," I said, making a face at her.

"No, it's true," she said. "Pigs don't even have sweat glands."

"Really?" Chef Claire said, pausing from the sip of champagne she was about to take.

"It's true. Pigs don't sweat. They wallow," Josie said with the nod of someone who knew what she was talking about.

"I defer to your superior animal husbandry skills," I said.

We walked across the lawn and made good time making our way to the house. Josie and Chef Claire headed upstairs to my childhood bedroom while I stayed behind to chat with various guests waiting to use one of the bathrooms on the first floor. By the time I got to my room, Josie had already showered and changed clothes.

"Chef Claire will be out in a sec," she said, running a comb through her wet hair before tying it back in a ponytail. Then she checked her outfit in the mirror, a loose-fitting shorts and blouse combination that looked very comfortable. She tossed the comb on the dresser then sat down. "Much better. I'm ready to dance."

Chef Claire came out of the bathroom wearing a similar outfit.

"The bathroom's all yours," she said, glancing around for her glass of champagne.

I stepped under the cold water and felt better immediately. I could have stayed there much longer, but I had guests to entertain. I also had some work to do as soon as the sun went down. As I toweled off, several scenarios about how events might play out tonight ran through my head. I shrugged off the most disastrous outcomes and focused on the honeymoon and some of the conversations Max and I would undoubtedly be having during our travels. Fifteen minutes later, we made our way downstairs and back to the reception. On the way, we crossed paths with Max and his brother who were heading toward the house.

"Great minds think alike," he said, pulling me close before taking a step back to examine my outfit. He gave me a hug and a kiss then squeezed my hand. "I can't wait to get out of this tux."

"Use my room to shower and change," I said, then grinned at the best man. "Great toast."

"Thanks," he said, glancing at Josie. "But I'm glad I went first. I would have hated having to follow you."

"Aren't you sweet," she said.

"Oh, you have no idea how sweet I can be," he said with a leering smile.

"And then you had to go and ruin it," she said, shaking her head.

"Ruin what?"

"You'll figure it out," Josie said, then whispered just loud enough for me to hear. "As soon as you start walking upright."

I tried to calm the building storm by changing the subject.

"After his childhood, I'm surprised Max is still alive."

"We all are," he said, laughing. His eyes were glazed over, and he was doing his best not to slur his words. "Have I told you how proud I am to be your brother-in-law, Suzy?"

"Yeah, you may have mentioned it six or seven times," I said, grimacing from the clumsy hug he gave me. "The feeling's mutual."

"I'll see you back at the table," Max said, bussing my cheek before gesturing at his brother to follow him.

We headed for one of the bars set up along the edge of the lawn. Josie and Chef Claire grabbed fresh glasses of champagne. I also selected one and set it down in front of me on the bar.

"I think I'm still dehydrated," I said, then flagged down the bartender. "Could I have a club soda with lime, please?"

"You got it, Suzy," he said. "And congratulations."

208

"Thanks, Tommy," I said, beaming at him.

Chef Claire sipped her champagne and gave Josie a knowing smile.

"What?" Josie said, staring back at her.

"Max's brother. He had a shot with you, didn't he?"

"Maybe," she said, giving it some thought before nodding. "He is cute."

"But then he opened his mouth," Chef Claire said.

"Yeah, don't you hate when that happens?"

Chapter 22

Just before the first dance, I spotted Chief Abrams standing by himself at one of the bars. I gave Max a kiss on the cheek and excused myself from the table. The Chief saw me coming and flashed me a big smile.

"You look a lot more comfortable than you did a while ago."

"I am," I said. "This is more my style."

"Yes, I know," he said, taking a small sip of his beer. "But you looked beautiful in your dress, Suzy."

"Thanks, Chief. Are you having a good time?"

"I'm having a great time. Just not as good as I expected."

"What's the matter?" I said, surprised.

"My original plan was to get hammered," he said, laughing. "But I have work to do."

"Thanks to me, right? I'm sorry, Chief."

"Don't apologize," he said. "It needs to be done. You really think she's going to show up?"

"I do," I said, nodding.

"I wish you would let us handle it, Suzy. We'll have guys covering both entrances to the maze."

"No, I need some questions answered that have been driving me nuts," I said. "And you know how I get when that happens."

"I could probably ballpark it," he deadpanned.

"Good one, Chief," I said, grinning at him. "And if I get her talking, with any luck she'll confess. It would save you a lot of work."

"It would," he said, then turned fatherly. "But if you pick up the slightest hint the situation is going to turn dangerous, I want you to get the heck out of there and find a good hiding spot in the maze."

"Sure, sure."

"I'm serious, Suzy. Just do your thing then get back to the party."

"Will do, Chief. Are you sure you're going to be able to find your way around in there?" I said, nodding in the general direction of the maze.

"I think so," he said. "I walked it earlier. But it's tricky to navigate if you don't know where you're going."

"Let me know if you get lost. I'll come and find you," I said, then pulled him in for a hug. "Thanks for being here today, Chief. It means a lot."

"I wouldn't have missed it for the world, Suzy. Now go do your first dance." He grinned and rolled his eyes. "Dazzle me."

"Yeah, I don't like my chances," I said with a wave as I headed back to the table.

I sat down next to Max, and he studied my face closely.

"Is the Chief all set?"

"He is," I said, glancing up at the stage where the band was ready to go.

"I really wish you'd give this one a pass," he said softly.

"I know you do, Max. But I'll be fine."

"And careful, right?"

"Do you think I'd do anything stupid to ruin our wedding day?"

"Rhetorical, right?"

I gently punched him on the shoulder and took another look at the stage where Reggie was trying to catch my eye. I nodded we were ready, and he approached the microphone.

"I'd like to invite Suzy and Max to honor us with their first dance," Reggie said. "And they wanted me to mention all of you are invited to join them. Suzy and Max, this one is for you."

He began playing the familiar opening riff on his acoustic. I grabbed Max by the hand and pulled him to his feet.

"I'm not sure I'm going to be able to move around much," he said.

"Don't worry about it," I said. "Save your strength for later."

The rest of the band joined in, and the song took flight. We began to dance, if what we were doing could be called dancing. Max was doing a limping-shuffle in a small section of the dance floor as I circled him swaying my shoulders and wiggling my lower half as we sang along.

"Remember the night we decided to use this song?" I said.

"I do."

"Don't repeat yourself, Max. You already used the line today," I deadpanned with a grin.

"That was a good night."

"They're all good," I said, picking up the pace as the band kicked into overdrive when the chorus began.

The night in question was the same day when my mother and I had again *discussed* possible first dance choices. After sticking a pin in the Sinatra option, I had gone home agitated and brought it up as soon as Max and I had gone to bed. As much as we both liked Frank, we agreed he wasn't a good fit. Then we started reminiscing about music. It wasn't long before we landed on The Tragically Hip, one of our all-time favorite bands. Canada's band. A band we still couldn't believe hadn't caught fire in the States. I'd been a huge fan for years, my fandom initially fueled in large part by the fact they were originally from Kingston, a city across the River not far from Clay Bay. Despite the fact they had never achieved the level of success here they should have, they were very popular in many other countries. But popular didn't begin to explain how they were perceived in their home country. In Canada, The Hip were rock-royalty. But with the passing of their lead singer, Gord Downie, a few years ago, a tragic day that produced, on a national level, the same reaction as my mother's tribute to Charlie Merrihew had a few hours earlier, the curtain closed on The Hip for the last time.

Max and I had spent the next few hours listening to various selections from the band's catalog and reviewing their lyrics. We eventually decided on *Ahead By A Century*, for me, a love song about two people trying to find their way in the world and finally realizing they only had one shot to get it right.

I looked at Max and he grabbed my hands. We began moving in a small circle as I continued to bounce and sway.

"No dress rehearsal, this is our life," I sang to Max with an enormous grin.

Max winked at me when I caught his eye. We picked up the pace and ignored the sweat streaming down both our faces.

"You are ahead by a century, you are ahead by a century, you are ahead by a century," we sang loudly to each other.

I waved to the rest of the wedding party, and they immediately joined us. I kept waving, and soon the dance floor was a jumbled mosaic of dancing, bouncing partygoers sharing the moment with those around them while solitarily enjoying memories the music was pulling to the surface. I caught a glimpse of my mother who was sitting nearby holding hands with Paulie. The smile on her face couldn't match the one I was wearing, but it had to be close. She raised her glass in salute. I silently mouthed an *I love you* to her then the music took me away again.

Josie and Chef Claire weaved their way through the throng until they were right next to us and the three of us bounced and swayed as we circled Max with our arms flailing in the air. We continued to beam at each other and sing at the top of our lungs. We sang to the memory of The Hip and the joy they'd given us over the years. We sang to the memory of Gord. We sang to our friendship. And we sang to our futures. It was one of those rare times in life when you wish you could stop time and replay the moment as long as you wanted on a loop.

I knew the first part of my life was officially coming to a close, but this was one hell of a way for it to go out.

I glanced up at the stage, caught Reggie's eye, and he grinned at me. I flashed him a quick thumbs up then tilted my head back and closed my eyes as I continued to squeeze Max's hands and sang like it was the last chance we'd ever have to do it.

"You are ahead by a century – this is our life - you are ahead by a century – this is our life- you are ahead by a century. And disappointing you gets me down."

Chapter 23

We danced two more songs before slipping away from the dance floor. Max led me by the hand through the dancers. We both chugged cold water before I gave Max a small wave and felt his eyes on me as I walked toward the Chief. He merely nodded and headed for the back entrance of the maze, a couple hundred feet away from where I was standing. I took a quick look around the party, didn't see the person I was looking for and took it as a good sign. I strolled casually toward the front entrance to the maze and soon found myself surrounded on all sides by the manicured hedges towering over me. I worked my way through the complex pattern and came to a stop when I reached one of the entrances to the sitting area. The fountain in the center was gurgling contentedly, and I flinched when I spotted the woman sitting on one of the benches. She was leaning back smoking a cigarette and had her legs stretched out, crossed at the ankles.

"Geraldine," I said as I approached.

"Hey, Suzy," she said, pulling her legs in to give me room to walk past her. "You were dancing up a storm out there. Remember when we used to bounce around the same way in your room?"

"I do," I said, sitting down across from her. "We had some great times."

"What are you doing out here?" she said, crushing out the cigarette with her sandal. "Taking a little trip down memory lane?"

"I'm supposed to meet somebody here."

"You need me to leave?"

"There's no need," I said, shaking my head. "Are you still mad at me?"

"No. I'm not mad. Just a little disappointed."

"I wish I could take our conversation back," I whispered. "Disappointing someone you care for is the worst. I'm sorry, Geraldine."

"Ancient history," she said, waving it off.

"Are you having a good time?"

"I am. It's a great party," she said nodding. "At least as good as I can have given what happened to my dad. The past few days have been a flood of memories. And a lot of them not good."

"Yeah, I get it."

"You meeting Max out here for a little private rendezvous?"

"I wish," I said, grinning at her. "Speaking of romance, I think I've figured out who you're having the affair with."

"I bet you a quarter you haven't."

The quarter bet was something we often did when we were kids. I smiled at the memory.

"I hate taking your money, but you're on."

"Okay, Smarty-pants, who is it?"

"Juan Jameson."

Stunned, she stared at me and shook her head.

"How the heck did you know?"

"It took me a while. I started thinking about it after I learned you weren't in Toronto to see *Hamilton*. The show hasn't even opened in Toronto yet. That's what initially got me thinking you might have been the one who killed your dad. It seemed logical at the time. Why else would you need a cover story, right?"

"Let's not go through it again, Suzy."

"Sorry. You mentioned before you were going home to L.A., you were heading to Boston and Baltimore. It made perfect sense at the time. You must have clients all over the place."

"Yes, I do. But how did it help you figure it out?"

"It was the day you stopped by the Inn, and we were watching the Yankees game. Juan was at the plate, and you couldn't take your eyes off the screen."

"He is gorgeous," she said with a grin.

"Yeah, he's definitely easy on the eyes," I said. "But he struck out, and you said he needed to learn not to chase the slider on the outside corner."

"I gave myself away, didn't I? It's hard to imagine me as a baseball fan, huh?"

"You always hated sports. I had a hunch but decided to check the Blue Jays schedule. After you spent the night in

Toronto with him after the game, they headed out on a road trip. After New York, they go to Boston then Baltimore."

"Well done," Geraldine said. "I'm impressed."

"Thanks. How did you meet him?"

"He's a collector of antiquities," she said. "His financial planner, a guy I went to college with, finally convinced Juan to start spending his money on something other than cars and jewelry."

"Well, he can certainly afford it," I said.

"Yeah, thirty million a year buys a lot. And it just took off from there."

"I hope it works out for you," I said, then frowned.

"But you have your doubts?"

"It doesn't matter what I think," I said. "It's your life, Geraldine. I just hope you don't spend years chasing a dream that might not happen."

"No dress rehearsals, huh?"

"Nope. There certainly aren't," I said.

"I'm still wondering why you came out here."

"I'm expecting someone, but she must be running late," I said. glancing around. "What do you know, there she is. Hey, Séance. Come on in."

"This maze is nuts," Séance said, shaking her head. Her eyes were glazed and unfocused. "I got lost back there and began to wonder if I was ever going to find this spot.

"Speaking of someone spending years fruitlessly chasing down a dream," Geraldine said, glaring at the actress.

Séance scowled at Geraldine then glanced back and forth at us, thoroughly confused. Then a lightbulb went off. She gave us a knowing but dark smile.

"Okay, now I get it," Séance said, slowly removing a small pistol from her pocket. "Co-conspirators. One to steal it, one to sell it."

"What on earth do you think you're doing?" Geraldine said, staring at the gun.

"Investing in my future," Séance said, sitting down on one of the benches. She placed the gun in her lap but continued to hold it with one hand. She was wasted and fading fast. "You know, I almost didn't make this trip. Heading up to this wasteland to attend some outdated societal ritual." She glanced at me and gave me a small shrug. "Sorry. But the idea of marriage is abhorrent to me. No offense."

"None taken," I said.

"Billy had to beg to get me to change my mind. And if he hadn't gotten the call from his father, I probably wouldn't have come. But I'm sure glad I did now."

"Do you know what's she talking about?" Geraldine said, glancing over at me.

"Unfortunately, I do," I said, nodding. "Séance murdered your dad."

"What?" she said, stunned.

"Murder's such an awful way to describe what happened. It was *almost* an accident. And it certainly wasn't my intention. Things happened so quickly," Séance said, then trailed off into a whisper. "But it doesn't make any difference."

"Why on earth would you want to kill my dad?" Geraldine said, still trying to make sense of what she was hearing. "You didn't even know my father."

"Only by reputation," Séance said. "Turns out, it was enough. He was very rude to me."

"You poor baby," I said, sneaking another peek at the gun.

She looked uncomfortable holding it, and I hoped her experience using a gun was confined to a prop she'd used on stage. And from the way she was imitating a bobblehead doll, I was pretty sure she had a better chance of shooting herself than either one of us. But I wasn't taking any chances. Getting shot on my wedding day wasn't on my to-do list.

"Do you have it with you?" Séance said to me.

"It's in my bag at the house," I said, lying through my teeth.

"Have what with you?" Geraldine said.

"Don't play dumb, Geraldine," Séance said. "Did Billy tell you, or was it Ginger Rogers over there who clued you in?"

Ginger Rogers? I took it as a compliment even though it wasn't how she had intended it. Mr. Rogers, maybe. But Ginger? Not a chance I'd ever be confused with her on the dance floor.

"Are you off your meds, today, Séance?" Geraldine said.

"No, I'm fully dosed," she said with a laugh. "Anti-depressants combined with a Vicodin and a couple of cocktails is a killer combo. I need to remember this one." She laughed again, this one bordering on maniacal. "I don't have a clue how you figured it out."

"Suzy, would you mind explaining what's going on here?" Geraldine said.

"It's still a bit sketchy. But I'll do my best," I said. "One day in the City, Séance was listening in on a conversation Billy and your dad were having. And your dad mentioned something about having a valuable artifact in his collection." I glanced at Séance. "Am I right?"

"You are," she said. "The old man called to tell him he had finished putting his affairs in order and had something very valuable. Then he made it a point to tell Billy he was leaving it to somebody else. And he laughed and laughed and laughed. It was a cruel thing to do. Especially to your son."

"I can see him doing it," Geraldine said. "Dad always took pleasure from tormenting Billy."

"I remember," I said. "And it always bothered me. Billy didn't deserve to be abused." I glanced at Séance. "But as soon as he mentioned something valuable, you had to see it for yourself."

"I did. And I couldn't believe it when I saw it."

"Saw what?" Geraldine said, her voice rising.

"You really don't know?" Séance said.

"Did you recently fall off the stage and hit your head?" Geraldine said. "I don't have a clue what you're talking about."

"What do you know?" Séance said, her words starting to slur. "He didn't tell his daughter either. What a piece of work."

"Suzy," Geraldine said. "What is she talking about?"

"The Red Diamond Dagger," I said.

Geraldine frowned at me and sat in silence for a long time. Then she leaned back on the bench deep in thought.

"*The* Red Diamond Dagger?"

"You've heard of it?" I said.

"Sure. But like most people in my line of work, I always thought it was a fairytale. You know, a bit of folklore for the people who love the fantasy of the quick score or winning the lottery."

"No, it's very real," Séance said, waving the pistol in my direction. "And she has it."

"Let's back up a bit," Geraldine said. "You're telling me all these years my father had the Red Diamond Dagger?"

"Yeah," I said. "He somehow managed to get his hands on it during the war."

"Wow. The Red Diamond Dagger," Geraldine said. "What does it look like?"

"It's incredible," I said.

"Amazing," Séance said, drifting off for a moment.

"It has to be priceless," I said.

"Oh, I'm sure I could put a price on it," Geraldine said without emotion.

"Yes, I'm sure you could," Séance said. "What with you being the bloodsucker you are."

"I'm a broker," Geraldine said. "All I do is put buyers and sellers together. If I make some money in the process, what's wrong with that?" She shifted in her seat to look at me. "You have the dagger?"

"I do. At least for now. I was going to cut a deal with Séance before turning it over, but I don't think it's going to happen now."

I paused to make solid eye contact with Geraldine before winking at her. She gave me a tiny nod to let me know she understood what I was doing.

"It's not going to happen now is it, Séance?"

"No, I'm sorry. I'm afraid I'm going to insist on a hundred percent ownership. I've had my eye on this gorgeous brownstone in the City for quite a while."

"Where you and Billy can live happily ever after?" Geraldine said.

"Oh, yeah. Billy," she said, shaking her head. "I'm afraid I don't see much of a future with your brother."

"After he spent all those years supporting you?" Geraldine said.

"Hey, I've always been honest with Billy," she said. "It's not my fault he chose not to believe me when I told him I wasn't ready to settle into something permanent. And I obviously wasn't going to do something completely stupid like getting married." She paused to give me another small shrug. "But I'm sure you'll be very good at it. Sorry to sound so negative on your wedding day."

"No, keep going," I said. "You're on a roll."

"I think it's your turn to talk," she said. "How did you figure out I was the one who killed him?"

"It finally came together last night at the rehearsal dinner," I said. "Max was heading off to the bathroom, and I jokingly asked him if he needed any help. He said, no, I think I know where it is by now."

I sat back as I composed my thoughts.

"Really?" Séance said. "Your husband knew where the bathroom was. That's how you figured out I killed the old man?"

"No, it's what triggered things. Remember the day when you and Billy stopped by his dad's house?"

"I do," Séance said, obviously confused about where I was going with the conversation.

"You said you needed to use the bathroom," I said.

"It has been known to happen," Séance said, waving the gun for me to keep going.

"Chef Claire was using the bathroom downstairs, but instead of waiting, you said you would just use the one upstairs."

"So?" Séance said.

"Since it was supposedly the first time you'd ever set foot in the house, how did you know there was a bathroom on the second floor?"

Séance blinked several times in rapid succession. I wasn't sure if I'd caught her completely off guard with the question or if the booze and meds had fully kicked in.

"But you had been in the house before," I said. "And I know exactly when it was."

"Do you now?"

"Billy decided to take a boat tour of the Islands the afternoon Charlie died. But you begged off. Refused to go. You told him you had a migraine coming on and being on the River would only make it worse. During the time he was gone, you went to see Charlie."

"I walked up to the front door and knocked. You should have seen the look on his face when I told him who I was," Séance said. "It was a look of pure hatred. I guess the only thing worse than his son was the woman who made the decision to live with him."

"But you talked him into showing you the dagger?" I said.

"After I confronted him about it, he couldn't wait to show it to me," she said. "It was like he got some perverse pleasure showing it off before telling me he was leaving it to somebody else."

"Who did he leave it to?" Geraldine said, listening closely.

226

"Mary," I said. "As a thank you for taking such good care of him over the years."

Geraldine nodded slowly but said nothing.

"Mary? His niece? How do you know?" Séance said. "The old man wouldn't tell me. Said it was none of my damn business."

"It's in his will," I said, glancing at Geraldine. "I'm sorry I couldn't tell you we found it."

Geraldine waved it off.

"Where did you find it?" Séance said.

"It was in a sealed envelope in the back of one of the binders," I said. "I'm surprised you didn't find it."

"I ran out of time," she said. "And I freaked out when I heard people downstairs."

"You were in the attic with Charlie, right?" I said.

"Yeah, he was sorting through all his junk. He showed me the binders describing all the crap he'd collected over the years. Then he got the strangest look on his face when he finally showed me the dagger. It was so beautiful." She drifted away as the memory took hold. "I couldn't take my eyes off it. It was so...*elegant*. Not to mention incredibly sharp."

No argument from me. I glanced down at the bandage on my finger covering the seven stitches Josie had given me.

"I felt like I was holding history," Séance said, then glanced back and forth at us. "Does that make any sense?"

"It does," I said.

227

"One of the perks of my job," Geraldine said, nodding. "And then you decided to kill him?"

"No, it was nothing like that," she said, finally tearing up.

They appeared to be genuine. We both sat quietly while she composed herself.

"After he let me hold it for a few minutes, he asked for it back. I was about to hand it over when he took a step closer and got right in my face. He pretty much snarled at me. Said it was such a pity this was the only time a *skank* like me would get her hands on it. Then he started laughing at me and reached for the dagger."

"Then you stabbed him," I said.

"It was more of a reflex reaction," Séance said, talking to us but staring off as the memory took hold. "I was furious about him calling me a skank, and I sort of jabbed it forward to make him get out of my face. But I hit him in the neck and knew right away I'd hit a major artery. Blood started spurting like one of those lawn sprinklers on pulse. There was so much blood. He clutched at his throat then his eyes went wide."

"Did he fall down the attic ladder or did you push him?" I said.

"I pushed him," she said with a shrug. "By then, it was pretty clear he was dying. And I figured the fall wouldn't make a bit of difference. I decided to make it look like an accident. After I shoved him, I tossed a box of junk down, then climbed down the ladder looking for something sharp to explain the cut on his

228

neck. I found what looked like a bayonet and dragged it through the blood." Her eyes had grown even wider as she told the story and she exhaled audibly. "Right before he died, he was trying to say something, so I leaned down over him. But he couldn't get the words out. He just kept staring up at me with a weird smile. Then he did something I'll never forget."

"What did he do?" Geraldine whispered.

"He slowly raised his hand. It took his last ounce of strength to do it. His hand trembled but continued to rise until he got it a couple feet off the floor," Séance said, then paused.

"Then what happened?" I said, engrossed by the story.

"He gave me the finger."

Geraldine barely managed to stifle her snort. She shook her head and glanced over at me.

"My dad, huh? Defiant to the end."

"Yeah," I whispered.

"Then I heard people coming into the house and panicked. I grabbed the dagger and the scabbard and climbed back up the ladder into the attic. But I was so frantic I dropped the scabbard when I was trying to slide the dagger back in. Somehow I managed to kick it. I think it went under an armoire."

"It did," I said.

"I didn't have time to deal with it. I looked around the attic for a way out and finally found one of those metal-rung ladders you hang out your window. So that's what I did. But it was windy, and the ladder was swaying in the breeze. And since I'm terrified of heights, there was no way I was going to try and climb down holding the dagger or stuffing it in my pocket. I'd just seen the damage it could do."

"So you put the dagger in the back of one of the binders with plans to come back later," I said.

"Yes. And find the scabbard at the same time."

"But you managed to take the page from the binder describing the dagger," I said.

"I did," Séance said, her eyes now officially half-closed. "I wanted to do some research on what the thing was. And get a feel for how much it might be worth. It didn't take long. I searched *antique red diamond artifacts.* It popped right up on the first page." She stared at me. "That's how you put it all together?"

"There was one more thing," I said. "Billy told me you grew up on a pig farm."

"I can't believe he told you," Séance said, turning dark. "We had a deal."

"I don't think it's your biggest problem at the moment, Séance," I said, staring at her in disbelief. "After you went upstairs to use the bathroom you headed straight to the attic."

"Yeah."

"But the binders weren't there," I said. "Chef Claire put them in a cabinet downstairs after she found them. When you realized they were gone, you let loose with the bloodcurdling scream."

"I was so mad," Séance said. "And I react involuntarily to anger. Occasionally, it comes out as a scream."

"Well, it's a good one. You might want to consider a career in horror movies," I said.

"Not a chance," she said with a snort.

"You told us you freaked out when you saw the bloodstain on the floor."

"I needed to come up with some sort of excuse."

"At the time, we all thought you were being a big baby about seeing a little dried blood. But after Billy told me how you'd grown up on a pig farm, it didn't make any sense. I imagine you've seen all sorts of worse things in the slaughterhouse."

"I don't want to talk about pigs," she said, shaking her head. "Let's sit here quietly for a few minutes."

"Okay," I said, then frowned. "Why do you want to do that?"

"Because the band's on break. And as soon as they start playing, no one will hear the gunshots."

"Sure, sure."

"Good reason," Geraldine said, nodding.

"What is this place?" Séance said, shaking her head again, this time to clear the cobwebs.

"The maze? Oh, it's something my mom had built when I was a kid," I said, then pursed my lips when an idea popped into my head. "We had a lot of fun playing out here, didn't we?"

"Lots of good memories," Geraldine said, reaching for a cigarette.

"Mind if I have one of those?" Séance said, her speech pattern slowing even more.

"Sure," she said, tossing her the pack. "I never figured you as a smoker."

"They help me keep my weight down," she said.

Séance fumbled the catch, but the pack landed in her lap. She set the gun down on the bench next to her.

"You remember the game we used to play, Geraldine?" I said, maintaining solid eye contact with her.

"Which one?" she said, unsure about where I was going.

"Meet Me In the Middle."

"Meet Me In the Middle," she said with a smile. She gave me a small nod to let me know she understood. "Wow. There's a blast from the past. Great game."

The game in question was a combination race and scavenger hunt where all the players ran into the maze to collect items hidden in different spots. The objective was to find as many of the objects as you could without ending up hopelessly lost in the maze. The game ended when all the players were back in the sitting area and the person who'd found the most items was declared the winner. Geraldine had been a tough opponent.

"Do you remember how to play?" she said.

"I could probably ballpark it," I said with a grin.

We both glanced at Séance who was struggling to get her cigarette lit.

"You need some help?" Geraldine said.

"I can't get the lighter to work," she said, repeatedly flicking it.

"I think I've got some matches here," she said, reaching into her purse.

I watched closely as Geraldine located a pack of matches and got up to hand them to Séance. I took another look at the gun still sitting next to Séance on the bench. Geraldine moved in close and extended her hand.

"Here you go," she said, then dropped the matches on the ground.

"Klutz," Séance said, leaning forward and looking down between her feet.

"Meet Me In the Middle!" I shouted and made a dash for one of the back exits leading out of the sitting area. I glanced over my shoulder and saw Geraldine disappear through the one closest to where she'd been sitting. As I did my best lumber down the gravel path, I heard Séance curse loudly. But it was too late. Geraldine and I were long gone.

I made a quick left, two rights, then another left before coming to a stop to catch my breath. I knew Geraldine was probably already getting close to exiting the maze. I also knew that Chief Abrams had the maze secured by two state policemen at both entrances. I was about to make my way toward the exit at the farthest corner of the maze when I heard a voice a couple of hedges away. He was mumbling and cursing under his breath.

"Chief?" I said, keeping my voice low.

"Suzy?"

"Yeah. What happened? Did you get lost?"

"I did," he said, not sounding happy about it. "Are you okay?"

"Yeah, I'm fine," I said. "I think I know where you are. It's a confusing section of the maze."

"I think I've been going in circles," he said. "Where's Séance?"

"If she's smart, she's still in the sitting area. If she's not, she wandering around lost. But she's armed, so be careful if you happen to run into her."

"What's she carrying?"

"A small pistol," I said. "And she's hammered."

"Can you give me directions?" he said. "This thing is nuts."

"I can," I said, recalling the section of the maze he was in. "Face north, make your first left, then right, then make another left at the third opening you come to."

"Got it," he said. "How long will it take me to get there?"

"Less than a minute if you follow my directions," I said.

"What are the chances I'll run into her?"

"If she left the sitting area, I'm pretty sure she went back out the way she came in. You're on the other side of where she's at."

"I'm on my way," he said.

I listened closely to the sound of his footsteps on the path until they got louder. When I was sure he was heading my way, I glanced at the opening he should come through, and seconds later his head popped into view.

"Man," he said, shaking his head. "You must have spent hours lost in this thing when you were a kid."

"Now you know why my mom had it built."

"Did you get a confession out of Séance?"

"We did."

"We?" the Chief said, frowning.

"Geraldine was in the sitting area when I got there."

"Doing what?"

"I think she was taking a trip down memory lane," I said. "Her dad's death is starting to take its toll."

"You both heard the confession?"

"We did," I said. "And it was complete."

"I can't wait to hear all about it," he said, glancing back and forth in both directions. "Why don't you head out the back entrance? I'll see if we can find our friend."

"Okay, but be careful," I said.

Before I took my first step, I heard a sound coming from another section of the maze.

"What the heck?" the Chief whispered.

"It sounds like someone crying," I whispered back then held a finger to my lips.

We listened with our ears pressed up against the hedge.

"Séance?" I called out. "Séance, is that you?"

"What do you want?" she said. "And where the heck are you?"

"Someplace you'll never find me. Are you crying?"

"Yes, I'm crying," she snapped. "I'm still trying to *process* the fact I killed somebody." Another crying jag ensued. Séance stopped long enough to cough then wail like a wounded animal. "I'm tired, I just threw up scotch and what was left of my meds all over myself, and I have no idea how to get out of here."

"Do you still have your gun?"

"Of course I still have it. Why do want to know?"

"Because I'm not going to help you get out until you get rid of it," I said.

A long silence ensued. I assumed Séance was considering her options.

"No, it's okay," she said eventually. "I think I'll hang onto it for now."

"Okay, your call," I said. "But I should warn you the cops aren't going to be very pleasant when they get there."

"Cops? You're bluffing," she said with a laugh.

I glanced at Chief Abrams and shrugged.

"You're on," I said to him.

"Séance, this is Chief Abrams, and I can assure you that Suzy is not bluffing. All I need to do is get on my radio, and

236

you'll soon be surrounded by a whole bunch of cops carrying big guns."

"Really?" she said, her voice almost childlike.

"Why would I lie?" Chief Abrams said.

"Because you're a cop."

"I'm going to forget you said that, Séance," the Chief said. "But you should know you hurt my feelings."

I rolled my eyes at him. He shrugged and grinned. Séance began another crying jag.

"I want to go home," she finally managed.

"Well, get rid of the gun, and we can talk about it," the Chief said.

Another long moment of silence ensued.

"What do you want me to do with it?"

I made a throwing motion, and the Chief nodded for me to proceed.

"Séance," I said. "All you need to do is stand up and throw your gun as far as you can in the direction of my voice."

"Or I could just shoot you through the hedges," she said.

"You could try. But I think it's the booze and the meds talking," I said. "If you want to try and shoot me, go ahead. As long as you don't mind six state cops returning fire with semi-automatic rifles."

I glanced at the Chief to gauge his reaction.

"Good one," he whispered.

"No, I don't want that," she said, again sounding like a little girl.

"Nobody does, Séance," I said. "So stand up and throw your gun as far as you can in the direction of my voice."

"Okay."

We listened as she scuffed the gravel climbing to her feet. Then we heard a loud grunt and the sound of the pistol landing in the hedges behind us.

"Good job," I said to her.

"Now what do I do?"

"Why don't you sit back down and relax? The Chief will be there soon."

"I could use a nap," Séance said, sobbing again.

"You're not the only one," I said, stifling a yawn. I looked at the Chief who was about to start talking on his radio. "Could you do me a favor?"

"Sure," he said, lowering the radio. "What is it?"

"Could you take her out the back entrance? Let's not ruin the reception," I said. "And if you don't mind leaving the sirens off, I'd appreciate it."

"You got it," he said, grinning at me. "Consider it a wedding gift."

Chapter 24

By the time I made it back to the reception, the Midnight Ryders were once again in full throat, and the dance floor was jammed. Max was standing off to one side talking with my mom and Paulie. She gave me a dark stare, and I immediately knew what had happened.

"You told her what I was doing, didn't you?" I said to my husband.

"She wore me down," Max said. "How did it go?"

"Séance confessed and is currently being escorted out the back of the maze by Chief Abrams and several other cops," I said, then asked the closest bartender for a glass of club soda. I guzzled most of it and held out my glass for a refill. "She's a complete mess."

"Séance killed Charlie," my mother said with a sad shake of her head. "Why did she do it?"

"Money," I said, taking a sip of my fresh drink. I caught another glimpse of the look on her face. "Don't be mad, Mom. It's over. And everything turned out fine."

"We had a deal, young lady."

"You said I had to let it go until after Max and I got married," I said, doing my best to deflect. "Technically, the reception isn't actually part of the wedding."

My mother took several deep breaths. I glanced at Max as we waited to see if she was going to blow. But she exhaled loudly and pulled me in close for a long hug.

"What a piece of work you are."

"Thanks for understanding, Mom," I said, squeezing her hard. "And thanks for everything you did to make this an amazing day. I love you."

"Now you're just sucking up," she said, managing a small laugh. Then she let go and looked back and forth at us. "You two should probably get going."

"Good idea," I said, then turned to Max. "Are you ready to go?"

"Absolutely," he said, setting his glass on the bar. "Jim and Mary are waiting for us at the house."

I took a final look around the party. It was pretty clear it would be going for hours. I almost hated to leave.

"Have you seen Josie and Chef Claire?"

"They're at the house with Jim and Mary."

"Okay," I said. "Let's do this."

I gave Paulie a long hug.

"Congratulations," he said. "Have a wonderful honeymoon."

"Thanks, Paulie," I said, then pulled my mother in close again. "I'll give you a call sometime tomorrow."

"You better make it sometime in the afternoon," she said, glancing around her lawn. "This place is going to be a disaster in the morning."

"You got it. You'll give our best to everyone?"

"We will, darling. Now go."

We did.

Max and I strolled hand in hand toward the house waving to several people on the way. I glanced back at the stage and gave Reggie two thumbs up. He grinned and nodded before refocusing on the music. We headed up the stairs leading to the verandah and found Chef Claire and Josie chatting with Jim and Mary. Luna hopped off Jim's chair and made a beeline for us. I knelt down to pet her then took a seat next to Max. The Wheatey trotted off and resumed her perch on Jim's lap.

"I swung by the house and picked her up," Mary said. "She loves being on the boat, so we figured what the heck."

"She's more than welcome," I said. "Aren't you Luna? How did you get in?"

"Josie gave me her keys," Mary said.

"I would have gone with her," Josie said. "But I had my hands full at the time."

"Ooh, sounds interesting," I said. "Dancing up a storm with one of the groomsmen?"

"She had her hands full of cake," Chef Claire said. "Her fourth piece."

"Third," Josie said, firmly correcting her. "And I'm sure I've already burned it off on the dance floor. But for the record, I have to say you outdid yourself with the cake selection."

"I'm so glad I didn't disappoint you," Chef Claire said, raising her glass in salute.

"Impossible," Josie said, clinking glasses with her. "Unlike men, cake never disappoints."

"You say the same thing about pizza," I said. I looked at Jim and Mary. "You guys ready to go?"

"Let's do it," Jim said as he set Luna down on the porch then got to his feet. "Your floating chariot awaits at the dock."

Chef Claire gave me a hug. I winced and grunted.

"Sorry," she said, laughing.

"You missed your calling. You should have been a lumberjack," I said, then pulled Josie in close. "Thank you." I took a step back to look at both of them. "Both of you. It was perfect."

"You're very welcome," Josie said, then shooed us away. "Now go. We'll talk in a couple of days. And don't worry about Chloe. We'll take good care of her."

"Thanks, guys," Max said, also hugging both of them. "You've been fantastic throughout the whole process."

"You're very welcome, Max," she said. "We couldn't be happier for you guys. Go. You're cutting into my cake time."

We followed Jim and Mary down to my mother's dock with Luna leading the way. Max climbed into the boat, extended a hand to help me in, and we sat down on the seat running the length of the transom. Mary untied the lines as Jim fired up the engine and the purr of the engine blended with the sounds of the party raining down on us from the backyard.

"It's a beautiful night to be out on the River, huh?" Max said, getting comfortable on the seat. He grabbed my hand and held it tight.

"It is," I said. "Feel free to take your time, Jim. There's no hurry."

"Will do," he said, slowly pulling out from the dock.

Luna raced to the bow and hopped up onto the seat. She placed her front paws on the top edge and surveyed the scene. The gentle breeze caused the fur on her face to flutter, and I laughed at the sight of her.

"It's like she's serving as a lookout," I said.

"It's her spot," Mary said, shaking her head with a smile. "She's such a good girl." Then her smile disappeared. "Séance is going away for a long time, isn't she?"

"I imagine she is," I said.

"I know Uncle Charlie was old," she whispered. "But it's still such a shock when someone you love dies. One minute they're here, the next they're gone."

"Yeah," I said, flashing back to the time when my mom had told me my dad had died. Nothing prepares you for devastating news like that. "I think Séance got caught up in the moment. The promise of the quick score. I think it ended up blinding her."

243

"It's the sort of crap that happens to people who live a life of self-absorption wrapped in a cocoon of fear and a longing for more."

"Well, look at you," Mary said, laughing. "Mr. Philosophical. Where did you come up with that one?"

"The back of a cereal box, I think," Jim deadpanned.

"Have you guys decided what you're going to do with the dagger?" Max said.

"Geraldine offered to sell it for us," Mary said. "She's even going to wave her commission."

Jim opened the throttle when we hit the main channel. We were heading downriver about five miles to Dancer Castle where we'd spend the night before being picked up in the morning by the yacht taking us to Montreal.

"Billy said he's thinking about taking Geraldine up on her offer to move to L.A.," Mary said. "Maybe what happened to Uncle Charlie will bring them closer."

"I hope it does," I said, nuzzling Max's neck. "I'm so happy," I whispered.

"Me too," he said. "And I can't wait to get to the castle and have you all to myself."

"Ooh, our first night as a married couple."

"It's gonna be a long night," he said, squeezing my thigh.

"Absolutely. We can sleep on the boat tomorrow."

The boat eventually came to a stop at the dock in front of the castle. Max and I climbed out and stared up at the massive structure.

"I've always heard this place is haunted," I said. "Is it true?"

"Maybe a little," Jim deadpanned as he set our bags down on the dock. "Mary, why don't you stay here with the boat? I'll get the happy couple settled in and be right back."

"You want to go back to the reception, don't you?"

"I imagine the party will be going for hours," he said, grinning at her. "What do you say?"

"I'm in," she said.

"Perfect," Jim said, grabbing our bags. "I won't be long. No, Luna, you stay here with your mama."

Max and I walked next to him as we strolled along the dock and up the path to the castle.

"You guys always seem so happy," I said. "How do you do it?"

"Oh, we have our moments. But actually, it's pretty easy," Jim said, glancing over at me. "As long as you marry the right person."

"No worries there," I said, squeezing Max's hand.

"Amen," Max said.

Jim gave us a quick tour of the first floor and introduced us to the night housekeeper. He escorted us to our room, made sure we had everything we needed, then departed with a promise to be back in the morning before we left. We surveyed the room and silently nodded our approval.

"You want to unpack?" Max said.

"I thought we might *relax* for a while first," I said, turning coy.

"Good call," he said with a wink.

He slipped off his shoes and flopped down on the bed. I stretched out next to him, gave him a kiss, then lowered my head onto the pillow. He draped an arm over my shoulder and pulled me close.

"What a perfect day," he said, stifling a yawn.

"Don't yawn," I said, also fighting fatigue. "It was perfect. The only thing left is for us to put a cherry on top of it, right?"

"Uh-huh," he said.

"As soon as you're ready," I said, having a hard time keeping my eyes open.

"Oh, I'm ready."

"Me too. And it's going to be an amazing way to end the day."

"Yup."

Two minutes later, still fully clothed, we were sound asleep and didn't wake until morning.

Chapter 25

After two nights and the morning of the third day, we arrived in Montreal on a gorgeous day. We thanked the captain and crew and piled into a taxi. We settled into the back and grinned at each other.

"You think you're going to be able to handle normal life again," I said.

"They did spoil us, didn't they?" Max said. "And I feel so relaxed. We should take the trip again soon. We can invite a bunch of people and take a week. I'd like to stop at some of the towns along the way and see the sights."

"Sounds great," I said. "You gotta hand it to my mom. She certainly knows how to put things together."

We checked into our hotel in the middle of Montreal's Golden Square Mile and decided to spend a few hours walking the city until it was time for lunch. I was taking Max to Le Pois Penché, one of my favorite French bistros. We casually strolled holding hands then heard the rumble of thunder.

"Oh, I hope it doesn't rain," I said, glancing up at the darkening sky.

"If it does, we'll just stay at the restaurant waiting it out and drinking wine."

"There you go," I said, swinging our arms back and forth as we walked.

"I think we should take another trip," Max said.

"Can we at least wait until after the honeymoon?"

"Funny," Max said, squeezing my hand. "I married a comedian. Yes, sometime after the honeymoon."

"Where would you like to go?" I said, suddenly on guard because of Max's fondness for the outdoors and physical exercise.

"I was thinking about Africa," he said. "On safari."

"You want to go to Africa and shoot wild animals?" I said, coming to an abrupt stop halfway across the crosswalk. "Don't you think it was something you might have shared before we got married?"

"Suzy, we need to keep walking," he said, gently pulling my arm. "C'mon, we need to cross the street before we get run over."

"Oh, sudden death," I said, standing my ground. "Like the poor elephants and lions."

"I'm not talking about shooting anything," Max said. "I'm talking about a *photo* safari."

"A photo safari?" I said, resuming my walk across the street. "You want to go to Africa and take pictures of wild animals?"

"Yes," he said, finally managing to get both of us across the street amid the blaring horns of a couple cranky cab drivers.

"You mentioned you wanted to do an exhibit in the rescue center featuring endangered species around the world. And I thought it would be great if we had some photos we took ourselves."

"Interesting," I said, nodding as we moved back from the street and made our way under an awning outside a cheese shop. "But I'm going to need a bit more, Max."

"I know you are," he said, laughing. "And I'm way ahead of you. Given your intense hatred for any sort of physical exercise."

"You weren't saying that last night," I said, cocking my head at him and raising an eyebrow.

"Fair enough," he said, laughing. "Nighttime exercise aside, you know what I'm talking about."

"I do. But hatred is such a strong word. Let's go with intense dislike."

"Fine," he said, smiling as he shook his head. "Given your intense dislike for *vertical* exercise, I've found what I believe is the perfect solution."

"A telephoto lens and a top-floor hotel suite at the edge of the savannah?"

"Unbelievable," he said, laughing. "Are you always going to be like this?"

"Rhetorical, right?"

"I married a goofball," he said, squeezing my hand. "Will you please let me finish?"

"By all means. Tell me all about this safari."

"It's great," he said, obviously excited about the idea. "It's a ten-day trip. And each day we drive about fifty miles. The people who run the company guarantee we'll see dozens of different species. Elephants, lions, gazelles, you name it."

"And the only thing we'd be shooting them with is a camera?" I said.

"Absolutely," Max said. "And we'll be in a jeep the whole time. The only walking will be whatever you decide to do."

"It's not so much the walking," I said, still not convinced. "It's the *running* from the wild animals I'm worried about."

"We'll be protected by the crew traveling with us," Max said. "And they'll be armed the entire time. You know, just in case."

"In case a lion decides I'd make a great snack, right?"

"Yeah, pretty much," he said, nodding. "But they've been in business almost twenty years and have never lost a tourist."

"Okay, good to know," I said, then another question floated to the surface. "But if we'll be trekking across the African jungle for ten days, what about the sleeping arrangements?"

"Well, since we're married now, I thought you and I would share a bed," he deadpanned.

"Funny," I said. "You know what I'm talking about."

"We'll be camping."

"Camping?" I said, my voice rising a notch as I stared at him. "Who are you?"

Max laughed long and hard.

"It's luxury camping," he said. "I'll show you the pictures on their website. They have these amazing tents. They're huge and very well-appointed. Each day, while we're doing our thing on the safari, a crew drives ahead to the place where we'll be spending the night and sets the camp up. They handle everything right down to the cooking and cleaning."

"And all we need to do is ride in the jeep and take pictures of the animals?"

"Pretty much," he said. "What do you think?"

"Well, I have always wanted to see Africa," I said.

"I know you have," Max said, gently squeezing my hand. "It sounds like fun, doesn't it?"

"Actually, it kinda does," I said, then exhaled loudly. "Okay, I'm in."

"Great," he said, pulling me in close for a long hug. "I thought we might go sometime early next spring after we get back from Cayman."

The rain began spattering the sidewalk, and I pulled him further underneath the awning. We huddled against the wall as the downpour intensified.

"Nah, it won't work," I said, shaking my head. "If we're going to do it, we need to go sometime this fall before Christmas."

"Why?" he said, confused.

I stared at him and decided this was as good a time as any to tell him.

"Because I'm pregnant."

He gave me a wide-eyed stare of disbelief then cocked his head at me.

"You're not joking around, are you?"

"Nope."

"But how?"

"Really? That's your question? How?"

"You know what I mean," he said. "How long? When did it happen?"

"It must have been right after I got back from my bachelorette party in Vegas."

"They were a couple of good days," he said, grinning. "This is fantastic news."

"I was so hoping you'd be happy," I said. "But it happened fast. You sure you're okay with it?"

"Okay? I'm thrilled," he said. "I can't believe it."

Thunder and lighting appeared directly overhead, and we held each other tight as a relentless rain hammered the canopy we were standing under. Max began to do a dance, and he bounced up and down on his feet.

"I'm going to be a father," he said, picking up his pace. "I can't believe it. And you're going to be such a great mom."

"You're gonna to be great too," I said.

"Have you told anyone yet?" he said, continuing his dance.

He'd never be confused with Gene Kelly in Singing in the Rain.

"No, I thought we'd wait until we got back from Paris," I said.

"Perfect," he said, grabbing my hand. Then he nodded and grinned at me. "Hey, that's why you haven't been drinking, isn't it?"

"I had a sip of champagne at the wedding."

"I should have figured it out," he said. "Your mother is going to be off the planet."

"I know," I said, laughing as he tried unsuccessfully to twirl me around. "Do you have a preference?"

"No," he said, letting go of my hand. "It's doesn't matter if it's a boy or a girl. As long as you and the baby are healthy, I'll be a happy man."

I continued to laugh as he picked up the pace of his dance, a combination of bad disco and a spider on a hot plate. He left the dryness of the canopy and was soon drenched from the storm.

"You idiot, come in out of the rain," I said, still laughing and having to raise my voice to be heard.

"It feels fantastic," he said, bouncing on his toes as he raised his arms over his head like Rocky.

Then he stumbled backward. His heel caught the edge of the curb, and he lost his balance. His momentum carried him into the middle of the road.

I will never forget the look of pure joy on his face before it transitioned into a mixture of confusion and surprise before eventually morphing into shock, a look forever frozen on his face and permanently carved into my head as a memory.

In the dim light and driving rain, the bus driver never saw him.

Epilogue

The next several weeks came and went in a blur of despair. Time passed grudgingly, almost as if the universe was doing everything it could to help me wind my clock back to the point right before it happened and do or say something to prevent the accident now haunting my waking hours and keeping my nights sleepless. The days were so similar throughout the entire time from Max's sudden and tragic death until today, a late-October day marked by a chill in the air perfectly matching the coldness in my heart, I could have easily been convinced the entire period was one, solitary endless day.

My first call, after I'd rediscovered the ability to utter a complete sentence without breaking into another extended round of sobs and howls, had been to Max's family in Ottawa. I then called my mother before continuing my conversation with the Montreal police. I checked out of the hotel, hired a car, and sat in the backseat bewildered and heartbroken as the driver made the trip from Montreal to Ottawa where Max's funeral would be held.

I was useless throughout the entire planning process and made it through the funeral in a shrouded haze with no lasting memory of what had happened at the memorial service or the cemetery. But I did discover being surrounded by Max's family, and soon my mother and Josie and Chef Claire, helped me get through what would undoubtedly go down as the worst week of my life. I discovered something else as well: Grieving in groups, while never easy for anyone, is still preferable to going through what I was alone.

By the time we made it home, I'd momentarily run out of tears. But I still hadn't found the need or the strength to eat. So I went to bed, comforted on a constant basis by Chloe and the other house dogs who instinctively knew something was very wrong. And I needed every ounce of salubrious love and affection they offered. The dogs also seemed to know something else was going on with me and studiously avoided jumping on my stomach when they hopped up on the bed. Occasionally, Chloe will rest her head on my stomach as she naps, then lift and cock her head at me as if she has heard something growing inside.

Josie immediately rented her new house, and she and Chef Claire moved back in. A week, then two, passed before I was able to drag myself out of bed for any extended period of time. Gradually, my daily life began to return to normal, and I was able to make it through a half-day of work without completely losing it. After four weeks, I finally felt strong enough to get through one of our regular Monday family dinners at the house without breaking down. And I let my mother and Josie and Chef Claire in on my little secret. Given the circumstances, their reaction, while one of surprise and delight, was muted.

When Chef Claire and Josie cleared the table and headed to the kitchen to load the dishwasher, my mother leaned forward and grabbed my hands and squeezed them gently.

"It's wonderful news, darling," she said. "You're going to be an amazing mother."

"Thanks, Mom," I said. "But I'm definitely going to need your help."

"Try and stop me," she said, laughing.

"Yeah, that's what I thought you'd say," I said, squeezing back before pulling my hands away to rub my forehead.

"Do you want to know if it's a boy or a girl?" she said, taking a sip of coffee.

"Already did it, Mom," I said. "I had a blood test the other day. It's supposed to be ninety-five percent accurate, but I've got an ultrasound scheduled next month to confirm it. I got the results back today."

"And?" my mother said, leaning forward.

"It's a girl," I whispered.

"I'm getting a granddaughter?" she said, tearing up.

"Yeah. A girl."

Josie and Chef Claire came back to the table and sat down.

"What's going on?" Josie said, glancing back and forth at us. "It looks like we missed something."

"It does," Chef Claire said. "What's up?"

My mother looked at me, and I gestured for her to tell them the news.

"Suzy's having a girl."

"Wonderful," Josie said with a shriek.

"Congratulations," Chef Claire said, getting up to hug me.

"We'll have to start thinking about names, darling."

"No, Mom," I said, managing a small smile. "We're not playing that game again. The first-dance song debates were more than enough."

"At least I'll have some input, right?" my mother said.

"No, Mom," I said, shaking my head at her. "You won't. I've already picked her name out."

"Okay," she whispered, obviously hurt but doing her best not to show it. "It's your baby."

"And there was only one name I could give her," I said.

I glanced at Josie, and she gave me a knowing smile. I still can't get anything past her.

"Her name has to be a tribute to the memory of her dad as well as a tribute to her beloved Grandma," I said, staring at my mother. "And there's only one choice."

"No, you're not," my mother said, tearing up. "Really, darling?"

"His name sits right inside yours, Mom," I said. "And I can't think of a better way to make sure she always remembers both of you."

"Maxine," my mother whispered, then started bawling into her coffee. "Thank you, darling. What a wonderful gesture."

"Little Max," Josie said, nodding. "I love it."

"It's perfect," Chef Claire, barely managing to get the words out.

"And I also have her middle name picked out?" I said.

"You have been busy," Josie said. "Do tell."

"Joclaire," I said. "I think I might have made up a new name."

"You named her after Josie and me?" Chef Claire said.

"I did."

"You're unbelievable," Josie said, raising her glass in salute. "I'm honored."

"Maxine Joclaire Chandler," my mother said. "It almost sounds like royalty."

"Don't get any ideas, Mom."

I turned the corner that night, but my path to recovery continued to be a slow, daily grind. And since there was no way I was ever going to be completely whole again, I doubted if I would even know when my recovery period had finished. But I pushed forward into October with my appetite definitely on the mend and beginning to show signs of my pregnancy.

Two weeks later, I headed down to the dock with Chloe leading the way. The sun was still below the horizon, and a stiff breeze was blowing out of the north. I was layered up and had my hands stuffed underneath my coat and sweatshirt. Rooster and my mother were idling into the dock, and Chloe hopped onto the front seat and said good morning to her as Rooster brought the boat to a stop and helped me climb in. Then he backed away from the dock and pointed the boat downriver.

"Are you ready to catch a big fish?" Rooster said.

"Rooster, we've been fishing for muskie for almost twenty years," I said, laughing. "And I've never caught squat. I don't even know why I bother."

"Because it's what we do, darling," my mother said, mildly chastising me. "In October, we fish for muskie. Next month, we eat turkey."

I watched the direction Rooster was heading and frowned.

"Where are you going?"

"I thought we'd try a new spot today," he said.

"Okay," I said, pouring myself a cup of hot chocolate. "You want some of this, Mom?"

"No, I'm good, thanks," she said, rubbing Chloe's head. "Did Josie and Chef Claire get off okay?"

"They did. They called last night after their flight landed in Rome."

Chef Claire and Josie had just left for a month in Italy where they would be traveling and studying local cooking techniques. Actually, Chef Claire would be doing most of the studying; Josie would be eating. Given what had happened to Max, they had originally announced their intention to postpone the trip, but I had talked them out of it. Reluctantly, they had eventually agreed, but only after being certain I had turned the corner on the grieving process.

Rooster continued to head across the River at an unfamiliar angle. He eventually slowed the boat and anchored. Chloe started to stir, but I stopped her with a firm command to stay.

"The last thing we need is you getting a fish hook in one of your paws," I said.

"She's fine," my mother said. "I'll keep a close eye on her."

"Aren't you going to fish?"

"I will at some point," she said, glancing around the immediate area. "For now, I'll just enjoy my coffee and this beautiful morning."

"It's forty-five and windy, Mom," I said, laughing as I reached for a fishing pole. "I'm going to try the Daredevil lure you gave me for Christmas last year."

"Good call," Rooster said. "Buddy Bannister told me about this spot. He said there's a shelf that extends out about thirty feet below the surface where muskie love to feed early in the morning. But if we don't have any luck being anchored, we'll start trolling in about an hour."

"Got it," I said, heading for the stern. "Why do I even do this?" I casted then slowly began reeling my line in.

"You know," Rooster said, also casting and sitting down with his legs stretched out. "There's an old Native American saying."

"This ought to be good," I said, glancing at my mother.

"No, I'm serious," he said as he continued to focus on the water in front of him. "It might even be a legend."

I reeled my line in, checked the lure, then cast again.

"Nice cast, darling," my mother said. "Your father taught you well."

"Well, since I know I'm not going to catch anything, I might as well work on my technique. So, what does this Native American legend say?"

"It says the first muskie you catch in your life contains the soul of a departed loved one," he said.

"Thank God for catch and release, huh?" I said, laughing. "You wouldn't want to be stuffing and hanging Uncle Albert on your wall."

"No, I'm serious," Rooster said. "According to the legend, it's one of the ways the loved one manages to say their final goodbyes to you."

"Good story. The Native Americans say that, huh?" I said, casting again. "Which tribe?"

"I'm not sure," Rooster said. "Buddy told me, but I forget."

"Were you guys drinking?"

"Of course," he said, casting again. "How do you think I got him to tell me about this spot?"

I felt a hard tug, and my pole bent at an angle toward the water.

"Wow," I said, tightening my grip on the pole. "Something big just hit my line."

"Take your time," Rooster said, setting his pole down and reaching for a net. "Take your time."

"I think I'm okay," I said, concentrating hard as I let the fish run a bit before starting to reel it in. "Geez, whatever it is, he's not happy at the moment."

"He just ate something that didn't agree with him," Rooster said. "Bring him in. Easy does it."

"Thanks, Coach," I said, glancing over at him. I continued to reel my line in and eventually got my first look at him. "I can't believe it. It's a muskie."

"It's a *big* muskie," Rooster said. "Maxine, you got your phone? We're gonna want a picture of this."

I managed to get the fish next to the boat and Rooster expertly scooped it into the net and out of the water. I set my pole down and stared in disbelief then glanced back and forth at Rooster and my mother.

"Keep him in the net and off the deck," Rooster said. "We don't want him hurting himself if he starts thrashing around."

"Not to mention the damage he could do to us," I said, feeling the full weight of the fish. "What a bruiser."

"Well done, darling," my mother said, keeping a hand on Chloe's collar as she leaned forward to hand Rooster her phone.

"Beautiful fish," he said, snapping a photo, then several more in rapid succession. "Let me measure him before we put him back."

He slid the phone into his pocket and used both hands to spread the measuring tool. I continued to hold the fish firmly to keep it as calm as possible.

"Almost fifty inches," he said, impressed. "Nice. Probably puts him somewhere around forty pounds."

"I can't believe it," I said, still stunned by my good luck. "Let's get him back in the water."

"You want a hand?"

"Yeah, probably a good idea," I said, then caught a glimpse of Chloe who was doing her best to inch closer for a better look. "No, Chloe. Stay."

"Can you see the hook?" Rooster said, holding a pair of needle-nose pliers.

"I can. He didn't swallow it. I think you can get it out without too much trouble," I said, using both hands to keep the fish's head as still as possible. "Let's get the hook out. He's been out of the water over a minute. We need to get him back in."

Rooster used the pliers to grab the treble hook. He expertly removed it without doing any more damage and attached the lure to my pole.

"Okay, let's keep him in the net when we put him back in the water. You might need to hold his belly until he resuscitates."

"How long will it take?"

"Not long. Ten, twenty seconds," Rooster said. "Don't worry, he'll let you know when he's ready to go."

I leaned over the side of the boat, and Rooster held the net while I supported the muskie's weight. The fish seemed to relax as soon as it was back in the water. I admired its markings and thick girth as I continued to hold it with both hands. I glanced at its large eye with a pulsing, black pupil.

Then the fish winked at me.

And it wasn't a quick blink of the eye. It was definitely a wink lasting at least two seconds. The muskie left the net with one powerful thrust of its tail and disappeared from sight. I continued to stare into the water, dumbfounded by what had happened.

"Are you all right, darling?" my mother said, a touch of concern in her voice.

"I'm fine, Mom," I said as I sat down on one of the seats. I shook my head to clear it.

"What on earth is the matter?" she said.

"The fish winked at me," I said, glancing back and forth at them. "I can't believe it."

"You sure it wasn't just blinking from the ordeal?" Rooster said. "Fish are known to do it when they're under stress."

"No, it was definitely a wink. The fish made solid eye contact and gave me a deliberate wink. I'm positive."

"Weird," Rooster said, then rubbed his forehead. "Hey, wasn't Max always winking at you?"

"He was."

"Darling, you really don't think…" she said, before trailing off, unable to finish the comment.

"I have no idea, Mom," I said, taking a final look down into the water. "But I'm gonna count it."

www.ingramcontent.com/pod-product-compliance
Lightning Source LLC
Chambersburg PA
CBHW070728280626
47159CB00023B/2872